continued . . .

Ace Books by Patricia Anthony

COLD ALLIES
BROTHER TERMITE
CONSCIENCE OF THE BEAGLE

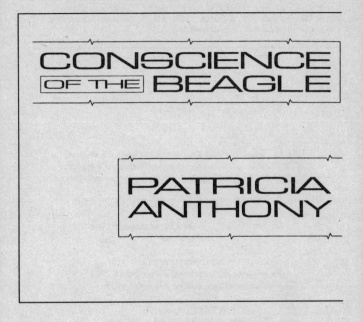

CONSCIENCE OF THE BEAGLE

PATRICIA ANTHONY

ACE BOOKS, NEW YORK

This Ace Book contains the complete text of the original hardcover edition. It has been completely reset in a typeface designed for easy reading, and was printed from new film.

CONSCIENCE OF THE BEAGLE

An Ace Book / published by arrangement with
First Books

PRINTING HISTORY
First Books hardcover edition published 1993
Ace paperback edition / October 1995

ISBN: 0-441-00262-5

ACE®
Ace Books are published by The Berkley Publishing Group,
200 Madison Avenue, New York, NY 10016.
ACE and the "A" design are trademarks
belonging to Charter Communications, Inc.

PRINTED IN THE UNITED STATES OF AMERICA

10 9 8 7 6 5 4 3 2 1

For the Wednesday Night Weirdoes.
Get out the likeastones, guys.
It's Chapter One.

1

I hate it when he smiles, as if we share a secret. As if, when he puts his hands on me, we'll both think it's fun.

His body's squat, genetically designed for the tidal forces near the singularity's rim. I could never take him on. There's enough muscle in those shoulders to subdue me if I struggle. Enough power to bludgeon me to death.

"We're pleased to have you aboard, Major Holloway. Our ETA for Tennyson is eleven days, seven hours, RES time. My name is Lawson, and I'll be your steward."

I hate that he knows my name. I resent him giving me his. Lawson My Steward has a voice that could be used as a lubricant. Or an emetic.

Planning escape routes is habit. I look for possibilities now. To my right rows of bubbles sit open, the nude men waiting in them like passengers on the half shell. Down the long row to my left the bubbles are closed and pearly with emollient.

"We're ready for the mask," Lawson says. "Hold your breath for a count of twenty. If the airway fails to open, let me know."

In one swift move, he smothers me.

"Just relax."

Blind, cold panic. I try to tear off the mask. Lawson looks astonished. He seizes my wrists. Must have never imagined that I'd fight him.

"It's all right. I'm here. I'm right here." His tone is soothing. His grip hurts. "Come on. You've been through this before."

They must have given him my dossier. The government is clever like that. A policeman, Lawson's thinking. Why isn't he more professional? Eight trips. Why isn't he used to this?

Never been so afraid. But I can't help it. This time something's wrong.

I forgot to count. That's what it is. How many seconds has it been? More than twenty. Has to be more than twenty.

Twin pops in my frontal sinuses. A welcome rush of air. Ashamed now, I go limp. Lawson's fingers have left red cuffs on my wrists. Tomorrow they'll be bruises.

"We're ready for the tube, Major Holloway."

He's no longer smiling. The urinary tube's in his hand.

I turn my head away to let him know that I won't resist. Lawson rolls the condom over my penis. The Smart Plastic is hot, its grip tight. I dig my fingernails into my palm. Count backwards from one hundred. Think of the victims on Tennyson. Nothing helps.

Lawson says quietly, "It's all right, Major. I see it all the time. Erections happen sometimes with tubal coupling. The sedation will take effect in a minute or two and it'll all be over."

I look around to see if anyone's watching. The other

passengers stare straight ahead, blank-faced, made self-absorbed by fear.

Lawson's so quick that I don't see him do it. The whoosh of the closing bubble catches me utterly by surprise. The world fogs. Trapped. Something thick, warm, and wet spills over my ankles. The emollient.

Damn it! Wait!

Lawson didn't warn me it was coming. Didn't want a scene. I thrash. My back spasms from hip to shoulder blade so painfully it feels like I've been shot.

I batter my fists against the walls of the bubble. Loud, so the other stewards can hear. They'll get me out. They'll realize I'm still awake. They'll get me out.

No, I'll drown—Pale bloated corpse. Bruises on knuckles like defensive wounds.

No! Please!

The screaming in my brain lowers to a whisper.

Please.

My eyelids twitch.

In the closet-sized kitchen of our apartment, Lila turns. Her smile is dying. Dying.

"Tell me about the murders, Dyle."

I don't know if she means the victims on Tennyson or if she's talking about another case. The acts of violence, a lifetime career of them, run together like thick red ink on a bone-white page.

I try to touch her, but my arm is tired from eighteen months of reaching.

"The murders are horrible," I tell her, and then I wonder if I've misspoken and my clumsy mind, my clumsy mouth have said, "Your murder was horrible." I must not have, though, because her smile doesn't change.

Something thick, warm, and wet licks at my chin. When it reaches my lips I'm afraid it will taste of salt and tarnished metal. And suddenly there I am, standing in the narrow corridors of M-4 SubLevel T Chicago, not far from home. Everything here is silent.

The floor is striped with the dot-dash-dot reflection from ceiling light tiles. At the end of the hall, where the tiles have failed, something patient waits in a pool of shadow.

Darkness pulls me. I bolt, but it tugs at my back. If I turn I'll see shadows at my heels. I run, trapped like a lab rat among the maze of tight corridors and the blink-blink-blink of the lights.

2

Someone's screaming. The sound bounces from wall to wall. It echoes along the corridor. And suddenly I'm awake.

A hush lies over the Jump recovery station. Dreaming, then. I wonder if I cried aloud. Around me, men slumber on tables like corpses in a morgue.

I hate the intimacy of travel. The helplessness. I hate knowing I was asleep while the stewards were awake. That once through the event horizon they carefully laid my body out, like some murderers display their victims.

Next to me Szabo dozes, a blanket pulled up to his chin. I have to be careful. HF is shrewd. When an investigator reaches the end of his usefulness, they send a spy. Who better than a psychic?

It could be any one of them. I don't know the team well enough: not Szabo the affable, not Arne the high-strung, not Beagle of the eternal life.

As I wait for a steward, I rub precipitate from my fingers. It comes away in greasy white rolls. When I look at Szabo the second time, I find him staring.

A steward has haphazardly cleaned Szabo's face. Pre-

cipitate sloughs from his balding head. His full beard is
caked with white. In that snowy chaos, his eyes are the
bright clear blue of mountain lakes.

Why is he looking at me?

He politely averts his eyes. Must have read my mind.
"I hate these trips," Szabo says. "You'd think you'd get
used to them after a while."

I greet the words with silence, the same deadly silence
that for eighteen months has settled in my rooms.
Sometimes I imagine I convey that silence like some people carry their kitchen's cooking smells in their clothes.

". . . prepared," Szabo murmurs.

I stiffen. "What?"

When he speaks his voice is casual, like he's hiding
something. "I hope everything's prepared for us down
there. I hate confusion."

"Major Holloway? You awake?"

Lawson's abrupt appearance makes me flinch. He leans
over, smiling.

"Let me help you up, sir."

His grip is gentle. Bruises on my wrists have faded to
bronze. My skin is forgiving. I'm not. If I wasn't so rocky
from the eleven-day sleep, I'd cold-cock him.

We don't speak. He takes me to a cubicle and leaves
me there. When I'm sure he's gone, I depress a white
button labeled SHOWER. A blast of hot soapy water
nearly knocks me down.

Outside my stall are coughs and mutterings, the noise
of running water, and shuffling feet. They are tired
sounds, disoriented sounds, as though the inhabitants of a
graveyard have awakened for Judgment.

Then, above my head, a ceiling tile flickers and goes out. I shouldn't look. It's not safe. I know that. But it happens so fast that it catches me off-guard.

There, just there. A black square in the ceiling, a neat hole punched into the universe. The giddy weightlessness of panic sucks me to it. My feet loosen from the floor. I reach out. Try to grab the tiles.

Just then I hear Szabo's gut-loud, merry laugh. Where did he learn to make a happy sound like that?

I close my eyes and hang on to that laugh. Hang on tight. It feels as though, having been flung into space, I've grasped a cable stretched between Earth and the stars.

3

Lila used to love the zoo. But memory fades, that's the good thing. Now I can look past Lila's profile and remember the aviary. Tennyson's groundport is as vivid, as deafeningly cheerful, as that.

Beagle sits on the bench beside me and leans over. His cheeks, his jowls sag on their frame. He has a cozy easy chair of a face. "They're fifteen minutes late," he says.

"I know."

"Are you sure we're not supposed to meet them at the hotel?"

A group of brightly-dressed colonials pass, three women and two men. All five stare at us. All five smile and nod. This time I don't get up. For fifteen minutes now, I've risen expectantly as colonials met my eye. Our brown-uniformed gloom must catch their attention.

I don't know which annoys me more: the scrutiny of the colonials or Beagle's challenge. "They didn't say which hotel we'd be staying at. The lodgings weren't arranged before flight time."

Beagle nods toward Arne. "His hands shake. Christ.

Think about that a minute. A demolitions expert, and his hands shake.''

I watch Arne pace. He's a small man, pale and fey, the sort of man best seen out of the corner of the eye.

"He's not regular Home Force," Beagle says. "They got him from the goddamned Bureau of Transportation and Commerce, and he acts like a head case. What did his files say?"

Odd question. Maybe a test. "You know those files are confidential."

Beagle's face might be soft, but his eyes are a hard gray. I wonder how much of Hoad Taylor lurks in them. "I'm M-8, Major."

No way I can have forgotten. M-8. And famous. I'm only M-4. I may be team leader, but in every way he ranks me.

I'm too cautious, too smart, to respond. He sits back and watches Arne. Why didn't HF choose Beagle? He must resent being subordinate. The strain of that resentment is bound to tear the team apart. Four-officer teams are unwieldy. Alliances form easiest in triads. If there's an odd man out, I hope to God it won't be me.

"You remember the routine Cully Blum used to do?" Beagle sounds amused. "The long involved one about the nervous rabbi at his first circumcision? The grandfather starts giving him instructions and, zip . . ."

I don't know enough about him. His files were strangely incomplete. So. Before he was downloaded into the Beagle, Dr. Taylor had liked Cully Blum. Did he have many friends? Was he married? Is his wife still alive? If she is, I wonder what she thinks of her living statue.

Beagle says, "Arne's the rabbi. The rest of us are dicks." He glances over my shoulder and clambers to his feet. "Company."

I rise and turn. Bustling toward us is a fat man. Grandly, flagrantly fat. The crowd parts. Like a ball, he bounces through.

He's the first human being I've seen on Tennyson who's not smiling. "You're late!" he cries.

Incredulity makes me hesitate. "What do you mean? We've been waiting over fifteen minutes..."

"No, *no!*" The man's rosebud mouth twitches. "You don't understand! You're *late!* You should have been at the hotel five minutes ago, and it's all my fault. Well, don't just stand there! Hurry, hurry, hurry."

And he's off, bustling through the crowd.

I trot to keep up. "Our luggage—"

An expansive gesture which nearly catches a well-dressed woman on the cheek. "All taken care of. The luggage is all taken care of."

The man's speech is rapid, and it has an odd colonial lilt. I'm not certain I've understood him correctly when he says, "Bedding."

"What?"

"Luxury bedding. A catastrophic docking. Simply catastrophic. Sheets and pillowcases in orbit. I don't know how we'll ever capture it all."

The doors slide apart. In the open, my steps falter. It's always disorienting, this first assault of the wind. The lack of walls. Sunshine dazes me. Beats warm on my face. I take a breath. The air has an intoxicating tang, but the light . . . Oh, the light. It's a commanding, majestic presence. It's the way, as a child, I always pictured God.

"So you can see, can't you?" The colonial herds us, blinded by the light, toward a cab. "You can understand the delay. Well, go ahead. Get in, get in. The cab's programmed for your hotel. I don't know how I let the time slip away like this. I looked at the clock and . . . They'll be very, very upset."

I climb into the front seat next to Beagle. The door slides closed.

The colonial peers in the window. "They're sticky about tardiness. It's covered under one of the major sins—sloth? Yes, must be sloth. Wouldn't fit under lust or avarice, I suppose. Just tell them it was my fault, will you? They're bound to ask. Well, go on. Go on!"

The cab lurches down the drive. Behind us on the sidewalk the man waves such an animated goodbye that his entire bulk quivers. "My fault, remember? Tell them it was all my fault so they know who to fine!"

The encounter leaves me stupefied. No longer certain of anything. "Did he say 'fine'?" I ask.

Sensing the lack of oncoming traffic, the cab makes its turn onto an eight-lane highway. In the distance crouch the low buildings of downtown Hebron.

Beagle chuckles. "Did you notice he never told us his name?"

"Look at the birds!" Szabo says from the back seat.

To our left is a rolling expanse. Lawn so perfectly green that it seems painted on. There willows hunch slope-shouldered about a pond and white birds sail like fat boats across its still surface.

"Ducks?" I ask, recalling Lila at the zoo and snowy birds on water.

"Swans," Beagle says. "My place has a view of a park, and they have a flock of swans there. I feed them sometimes."

Swans. A park. A pond. M-8 Level perks. I wonder if his apartment is on the top floor. If it's washed in cascades of sunlight.

Szabo says, "Aren't they pretty?" with such yearning that I wonder what he sees out his own apartment window.

"Fuck the goddamned swans," Arne says.

Beagle and I exchange looks. My shoulders untense. Arne. So the odd man out will be Arne.

4

No one is waiting for us at the Hebron Crossroads Hotel. Just inside, I slow my pace. The lobby is a forest. Vines hang Rapunzel-like off interior balconies and huge birds roam free down leaf-dappled walks.

Peacocks. I remember them from the zoo. I see them filtered through Lila's smile. The birds are peacocks.

Have they somehow gotten loose? I'm leery of them. Szabo trails a plain brown female through a stand of miniature orange trees, clucking to her, until Beagle asks if that's the way he gets dates.

Szabo laughs. So do three colonials sitting at a nearby table having lunch. So does the hotel clerk standing behind a marble desk. Privacy stolen, I fall silent. The colonials at the table grin as if waiting for us to break into song.

"You're all taken care of." The desk clerk holds up his hand, door cards fanned in it. He looks as if he's going to ask me to pick a card. Any card. "I've got your keys."

I walk over to the clerk. Ask in a low voice, "Where are the officials who are supposed to meet us?"

Only the innocent can look that blank, that confused.

"Nobody's come around. At least . . . you mean someone from the govern—"

"Yes. The government. They should have been here fifteen minutes ago."

"I had a message—"

"What does it say?"

"That four Earthers were coming. It was on my net when I came on duty. Management left it. I always get instructions when I come on—"

"No official message for us? Nothing? You sure?"

"No." I've frightened him monosyllabic. That fear. It happens when I look at people. It happens in the interrogation room where the intimidation is planned. In everyday situations where it is not.

"Fine. That's fine. If anyone calls, tell them we're here." I snatch the keys.

The clerk calls after me, "Sir? Would you like meal service to send something up to your rooms? Shrimp cocktail? A steak? You might as well. Tennyson's picking up the tab."

I'm walking toward the team when I see Szabo's sky-blue eyes widen. "I'd love a steak!"

"How do you want it?"

A bewildered hesitation. I'm confused, too. Such a luxury, a steak. How do you want it? Szabo might reply: Desperately.

"Well-done?" the clerk prompts. "Rare? Medium?"

"Oh. Yes. Medium."

Suddenly, Beagle walks to the banks of lifts. As if he's been made team leader by silent acclamation, Arne and Szabo follow.

On the eighth floor, I stand before my room's anach-ronistic Hilton Revival doorknob pretending to read the back of my key.

INSERT CARD IN READER. TURN KNOB TO THE RIGHT AND PUSH.

I wait until each member of the team enters his room. Until I'm sure that Beagle won't make another attempt on my authority. Then I go inside.

The room is huge, nearly as large as my apartment. I ignore the Wall and pull aside the sheers. Dazzling sun-shine bursts through.

Beagle. So the spy is Beagle. Arne's too volatile to manipulate and Beagle will ally himself with Szabo. I have to remember that whoever controls Szabo, controls the team.

I look down on the lush multicolored quilt that is He-bron and force myself to relax. The hidy-hole of a win-dowsill is my favorite place. When I was a kid, I would stare across at the smudged windows of the neighboring megacomplex. In all the years I sat there, no one ever looked back. That's the secret of windows. Looking out of them is like being invisible.

A warm clasp on my shoulder boosts my heart into my throat. Lila. Never could break her of the habit.

Don't come up behind me and touch me like that. Tell me you're here. Just tell me. Don't you know better than to do that to a cop?

I jerk my head around. But the room is empty.

Lila. The feeling of being followed leaps to its feet with me. I pace and it walks by my side. It watches as I stretch out on the bed.

The air's too thick to breathe. Have to get out of here. The lobby? No. Not with the laughing colonials, the birds. Only one escape makes sense. I walk down the wide carpeted hall toward Szabo's.

Five yards from his room I halt. A shudder in my chest so strong that my heart stops. Szabo's door is standing ajar.

Something's happened. I know it. I feel it in the thickness of the silence beyond; in the syrupy dark of the room. Don't have anything to fight with. Orders were to leave our softguns behind. Szabo needs me. And my feet won't leave the light.

From inside, a low cry. Another. Inarticulate mewlings of pain.

"Szabo!"

He's suddenly there. In the doorway. Safe. "Major?"

"Why the fuck did you leave your door open!"

Eyes round and startled. "I just—"

"God! Anyone could have walked in!" My head pounds so hard that my vision swims. "You're responsible for your own safety! You can't rely on me for everything. I can't be with you twenty-four hours a day. Jesus! A kid—I can understand a kid. They don't have any sense. But you? It's like you're asking to be murdered. Victims. I see shit like this all the time. Your own damned fault. You walk around in a fog. You wander out of crowded areas. If you stayed in a well-lighted place you'd be . . ."

God. Shut up. Shut up. But I've said too much already.

"Major? Are you all right?"

A hand on my arm halts my retreat. I shake him off,

swipe angrily at my eyes. Don't know him well enough
for him to see me this way.

"Come in. Sit down a minute." He grabs my sleeve
and pulls me into the room.

The air's heavy with the smell of food. An empty plate
sits atop an autocart. The Wall is playing a holo of a rocky
beach. The sky's a melancholy gray, the humpbacked
waves green. Strange how a sunny man can be this drawn
to shadow.

"Turn on the lights."

He hits a wall switch. The room takes color. Arne is
sitting near the Wall. His legs are crossed. Face rigid. Oh.
Arne won't be the odd man out after all. It will be me.

"Major." Arne sounds less than delighted.

"I didn't mean to disturb you . . ."

"It's okay." The psychic's smile looks painted on with
a mortician's brush.

Turgid silence falls. In that silence I hear the slap of
waves and the murder-victim mewling of gulls. Szabo
bends down and hits the RETURN button on the autocart.

"Were you finished?" I ask. Arne seems angry, as
though I've shattered some earlier, delicate mood.

"Sure," Szabo says, glancing to Arne. "All finished."

The cart makes a musical jingle as it negotiates the turn
into the hall. Then a thump. A dramatic clatter.

A curly-headed colonial in an expensive Slickstone suit
limps around the jamb. "Hi there!" He beams and rubs
his leg. "You must be the Earthers."

Do I look that out of place? Don't we all? Three brown
birds in an aviary.

"I'm John Vanderslice, the Minister of Science." He

shoves a presumptuous hand at me. He gives me no choice but to shake it.

"Have to watch that," he says with a laugh. "Leave your door open and anyone could walk inside."

He heard. He was hiding around the corner, just out of sight, all that time. Listening.

Vanderslice's face is swept clean as a vacant apartment. His green eyes are large, guileless, and in constant motion. "I'm supposed to bring one of you to meet His Excellency. Just one, though. Since you're team leader, it'll probably have to be you, Major. Marvin can't stand to be around more than one Earther at a time. 'John,' he says, 'you ever notice how they never talk? And they never look you in the eyes—ever notice that?—like they're shifty.' "

Drowned in a flood of speech, I look at Szabo. His eyebrows are knit. His fingers pause, arrested on his beard, mid-stroke.

"Marvin—The Chosen of God, that is—we grew up together. Used to make spitballs in elementary school before he got called to the ministry. Old Marvin, the spitball king. He hates when I tell that story, just hates it. But still, he made me Minister of Science, didn't he? It's because I know where all the spitballs are buried." He winks conspiratorially at Arne—why Arne?—and smooths the front of his jacket.

"So anyway, I tell him, 'Marv, that's just the way they are. Don't let it get to you.' Poor Marvin. He doesn't understand sociopathology. I would have gone into sociology if mother hadn't insisted on geophysics. She—"

Beagle enters the room so quietly that Vanderslice only

notices him when the construct is standing at his shoulder. He looks up, startled, into Beagle's frown.

I think he'll be prudent and step back. I would. But Vanderslice shoves forward a hand. Beagle automatically takes it.

"Dr. Taylor! It *is* Dr. Taylor, isn't it? This is such an honor, sir! I've only read one of your studies in statistical criminology. It's tough going, if you don't mind my saying so. Hope you'll take the time to explain some of the more esoteric concepts while you're here. I have the annotated *Paths Through the Jungle*. Brilliant. Simply brilliant."

Brilliant. The word casts me into shadow.

Vanderslice refuses to let Beagle go. He studies the construct's fingernails. His palm. "It's just amazing. Isn't it?" His Pied Piper enthusiasm lures Szabo into amazement with him. "Absolutely lifelike. Have you ever touched him? Warm and—"

A tug and Beagle reclaims his hand.

"Oops. I'm being rude, aren't I? Oh, well. We'll just have to get used to each other. I'm your liaison while you're here."

Liaison. Liaison. I twist the word this way and that but, like a kaleidoscope, only splintered images form.

"Just tell me when I'm being rude. You won't hurt my feelings."

In the background, Arne lifts a finger, takes a breath. If he's about to say something, he's too late.

"I'm used to working with off-worlders. You Earthers evade eye contact. That makes us think you're devious.

We tend to talk too much, and that gets on your nerves. Well.''

He falls disconcertingly silent. I find myself balanced on the balls of my feet, waiting. He rubs his palms together. Nods and grins. ''It was great meeting all of you. The Home Force sent me your files, and I feel like I know you already. So. Major. You ready to gird your loins and meet the spitball king?''

No way to avoid it. When he leaves, I follow.

5

Every other colonial babbles. So why aren't these people talking? Around the table the Chosen's cabinet sits in varying degrees of unease.

At my right shoulder a minister busies himself by alternately doodling flowers on his Sheet and tapping the erase button with his stylus. To my left Vanderslice folds and then unfolds a napkin.

The spitball king's puffy face, his rounded body, seem inflated by the pressures of self-importance. His small hazel eyes pick me apart. "So," he says at last. "The man who arrested Reece Wallace. Impressive." His voice is a surprisingly effeminate tenor.

All eyes, even those of the Minister of Doodling, shift. "Yes."

Vanderslice is the only one of the group who smiles. The others' apprehensive gazes dart to the man at the head of the table.

What have I said that annoys him? The Chosen of God scowls. His scowl continues long past where it should have stopped. It pulls the heavy lips down and down.

"I see you are impolite, Major. Earthers. So vulgar. So

full of yourselves.'' Marvin taps a manicured fingernail on the table. ''Well. In spite of that, we require a quick end to this thing. And I would hope you're bright enough to see through the gossip.'' Gossip? I glance around. No one is looking my way, and they are doing so pointedly, as if afraid my very eyes might damn them. All the cabinet but Vanderslice. The Minister of Science is atypically silent. His handsome face is daydreamy calm. It looks as if he has imagined someplace nicer to be, and then has escaped there.

''I want to know how you plan to proceed.'' The Chosen steeples his pudgy hands.

''Milos Arne will review the data on the explosions themselves. When he determines the certain-kill radii, then we hope our statistics man can find some patterns.''

''And then what?''

''I'll follow the patterns with our psychic. When it's time for the interrogations, I'll conduct them. I will conduct them alone, you understand. Without any help from the locals.''

I expect anger, but Marvin's rage explodes in an unforeseen direction. ''Is that it?''

''What?''

''Is that all you plan to do? Find your radii or whatever and then follow your nonsensical patterns? What if the explosions were random?''

''There is no randomness, sir. Terrorist acts and serial murders contain an internal motif. Finding that motif, no matter how absurd it appears on the surface, is what our statistical criminologist was a genius at. That's why he was constructed.''

"Abomination." The Chosen of God slumps. His belly forms a moat of fat below his chest. "Constructing a man. It's an abomination. I ask you, where is the soul in all of that?"

Beagle's soul. Is that why Yi named me team leader? No. HF isn't that diplomatic.

"I suppose you'd have to ask the construct, sir, and see if he has discovered his."

The Chosen of God shoots to his feet. The ministers cower. The man to my right stops doodling. He hits the erase button, then industriously writes at the top of his Sheet INVESTIGATION. He underlines this twice and stabs a colon on the end.

"A psychic and a construct." The Chosen's lips purse in disgust. "And you, like Lucifer, are rotten with the sin of pride. I wonder if you haven't made up your mind already." I tense as Marvin stalks his way to my side of the table.

The doodler begins writing furiously. Under INVESTIGATION: he prints LUCIFER? SOULS? The Chosen pauses to look at his minister's Sheet, sees that it is good, and walks on.

"Haven't you?" he asks me. "Haven't you made up your mind as to who is guilty?"

"May I ask a question here?"

Sullen silence from the Chosen. Alarm from the others.

"Was I misinformed? Or didn't you request our help?"

Everyone is looking at me, their faces, their bodies still. Marvin is standing so close I can feel the warmth from his body. I refuse to look up. Instead, I tilt my coffee cup toward me. There's a single swallow of coffee at the bottom, long gone cold. Some people on Earth would have killed for that swallow.

Then I notice, almost peripherally, that the Chosen's hand is trembling. "What religion are you, Major?"

What's scaring him? "Is that germane?"

"Are you afraid of my question?"

"Not afraid. I'm taken aback. I'm insulted. I normally don't think in terms of religion. I can't afford to."

"Afford to, Major? You mean you can't fit murder in the divine plan, isn't that it? You look at Earth's violence and wonder where faith comes in. Well, this isn't Earth. We're a God-fearing community. If you wish to solve these crimes, it would be best if you understood that."

The Chosen walks to the door. The ministers rise. I watch Marvin leave with all his retinue but Vanderslice.

"Excellency?" I call.

He pops back in the doorway.

"If your people are so God-fearing, why are they killing each other?"

I don't know if he lacks an answer or if he's too furious for speech. The doors shut on that extraordinary scowl.

Next to me, Vanderslice lowers his head to his crossed arms. His shoulders shake with silent laughter.

6

All during the ride down the lift, all during the walk to the limo, Vanderslice is mute. I recognize that silence. It's the same careful silence I keep in my office. Vanderslice thinks the building's bugged.

In the limo, we sit opposite each other. He opens a tiny refrigerator and, without asking if I want one, brings out a pair of native soft drinks. The soda is an off-putting hue of purple and sickeningly sweet.

I set the soda down. "Who's in charge of the local investigation?"

Vanderslice's head is tilted back against the seat. His eyes are closed. He has a sheltered, guileless face.

One eye opens. "Me," he says.

I suppress a laugh. Of course. That's why the investigation is stalled.

"The gossip Marvin mentioned. What is it?" If he thinks the car is bugged, Vanderslice won't answer my question.

He stops smiling. He studies the level of his soda. Tips the bottle this way and that. "You ever hear Marvin preach?"

I don't bother to answer.

"He's good. Really good. Marvin and I go way back, and he was always a star. While the rest of us were busy playing ball, he memorized the New Testament. When we were discovering girls, he'd already begun his ministry."

My attention wanders from Vanderslice's monologue. The limo's been moving at a brisk pace, and wherever I look are houses. Individual houses on their own private lawns. There are sidewalks, too. But no one's outside. Strange. If I lived in that neighborhood, I'd walk there.

"Marvin was one of those guys who knew where he was going. He was ambitious that way."

Ambitious. The word rouses me from boredom like a slap in the face.

"Marvin had the handicap of that voice. You've heard him. He sounds like a castrato. But otherwise, he was a natural. Straight-A student. The class cut-up. When we were in school, and the teacher wasn't around, he'd preach these hilarious sermons. He'd talk about sin and make his voice tremble. He'd talk about forgiveness and cry. Old Marv gave an outstanding performance."

I look out at the houses again. Lila and I could have been happy there. Maybe we could have had a dog. A small white fluffy dog like the kind she cooed over in pictures. My fault we didn't. Ten years as an M-4. Twenty years of successful cases and criticisms in my Personnel File.

Doesn't work well with others.

Prima donna.

Insubordinate.

The bastards. I should have been M-6 at least. I had the seniority for it.

Troublemaker.

Iconoclast.

I wanted to buy Lila that little dog. Wanted to live where ceiling light tiles never fail. But I didn't want it bad enough. We could have had an apartment on a restricted M-6 Level. A spacious apartment. With security cameras. Neighborhood security gates. She wouldn't have . . .

"You'd never know it," Vanderslice says.

I've clenched my fists so hard that my hands have cramped. Never know what? I'm lost. Nothing he's saying makes any sense.

"When Ed the Chosen died, Marvin managed five True Prophecies, three more than his closest competitor. He forgets how many times he was wrong. A few years ago he told me that when he opens his mouth, God speaks." The green eyes lift to mine. "I think Marv's crazy."

I stretch the ache out of my fingers. Vanderslice has finally come to the point. "So that's the gossip."

He leans toward me. Backlit by the morning sun, his brown curly hair is a halo. "No. Listen. If Marvin thinks he's the right hand of God, he has to believe in mercy."

Wide sidewalks, green lawns flash by. Marvin and Vanderslice were born here. Of course they believe in mercy. The people on M-6 might believe in it. On M-4 ceiling lights fail.

" 'Into Thy hands I commit my spirit,' remember? Marv takes that to heart. He'd punish a sinner. He's done it before. But he's absolutely incapable of hurting someone to save himself. No matter how many thou-shalt-nots Marvin's made of, no matter how inflexible or self-righteous or even silly he might be, God commanded submission. And Marvin isn't going to let Him down. Once you understand Marvin, really understand him, you'll see the conclusion my investigation reached is all wrong."

He pauses for my question, but I'm not interested in his answer. Vanderslice is gullible. Too sheltered to buck the system. I ask anyway. "So what was the conclusion?"

Vanderslice presses his lips together. Gives me a shrug that is more nervous tic. "That Marv is behind the terrorist acts. And the murders are part of a government conspiracy."

7

My mouth opens in astonishment. What? I want to ask.
What? But then the limo whines to a halt in front of the
hotel. The doors slide open. Vanderslice jumps out and
walks up the sidewalk to the entrance.

"Wait a minute!" He ignores me. Angered, I catch up
to him and jerk him around. "Wait just a fucking minute!"

"Oops. Watch that language." There's a bemused look
on his face. "Lucky there's not a God's Warrior around
here, he'd fine you."

The grounds of the hotel and the spacious sidewalk
where we're standing are empty. Along one side of the
huge hotel is a pine forest, a gazebo placed in it like a
shrine. It's empty, too. I don't understand these huge
places where nothing at all happens.

"What do you mean, 'government conspiracy'?"

A girl suddenly appears at my shoulder. If she had a
knife I'd be dead now. Her smile is bright, wide, and
vacant as the hotel grounds. A Bible is clutched to her
breasts. "The planet of Tennyson was colonized one hun-

dred and fifty years ago by Harold and Mimi Tennyson, of Earth . . .''

Where did she come from? How could I let her sneak up on me like that?

"When the God's Warriors started looking into the terrorist acts," Vanderslice says, "they probed the DEEP program in the net of one of the first victims, and found plans for a coup hidden in a subsub file. The Warriors got scared because this wasn't just some malcontent or blasphemer they were dealing with. This conspirator had status."

The girl prattles an upbeat counterpoint to Vanderslice's minor-key tale. ". . . could found a society free from crime and sin . . ."

Vanderslice doesn't look at her. Is she really there? Does he want to make me believe I'm seeing things?

"So that's when Marv asked me to take over the investigation, because the God's Warriors are just cops— no offense—and even Marv was starting to worry. You could nail him to a cross. He'd let you. But he never had any burning desire to be a martyr."

The girl stops talking. Looks expectantly· at me. I'm afraid to meet her eye, afraid Vanderslice will ask what I'm looking at. I don't know what I should tell him.

After an awkward pause she asks if I would care for any printed information.

"Tell her no," Vanderslice says.

Damn it. What kind of game is this?

Then he shoves his arm through the Bible, through the frilly dress, until everything past his elbow is lost from sight. The girl is still smiling.

"A Chamber of Commerce holo. She picked you out because you don't have an EPAT. Tell her no."

"No." So easy. Not murder, but something like it. The girl and her perky smile wink out of existence.

"EPATs. We're implanted," Vanderslice says, touching a tiny scar on his wrist. "Eternal Prayer And Tithe. HF told you, right? It tracks where we are every minute of every day. Being an Earther, that'll probably lead you to the wrong conclusion. Truth is, nobody cares. Nobody wants to know where an EPAT goes. We're God-fearing, trustworthy citizens, otherwise our EPAT would be taken away. It's the Banished out of Bosom that the government worries about. They're the ones they keep an eye on. At least until now."

Vanderslice has been tagged like a convicted petty thief. Why did he stand for it? Nothing could make me give up my freedom like that. "I'll want all your files."

He gives me a self-deprecatory nod. "Sure. I've already sent some to Dr. Taylor's net. I'll get you the rest right away. It won't be what you're used to, though. We're amateurs at this, and everything's pretty sloppy."

"Get me everything." I walk to the door. Vanderslice follows.

"Look, Major. Why don't you let me help you? There's a lot about Tennyson you won't be able to understand. I'll try not to get in your way."

Vanderslice would always get in my way. "*You* look . . ." I face him.

"John. Just call me John."

"It's nothing personal. I'm simply not allowed to work with any locals. In off-world cases, HF never shares information. There's too great a danger that the contact is implicated. Or that he's an informant.''

Vanderslice is crushed. "Oh. Sure. I understand.''

But when I enter the building, he's right on my heels.

The heart of the lobby is pierced by brilliant shafts from the skylights. Beagle and Szabo sit at a table under a waterfall of green vines. Arne's chair is pulled some distance from the others as if he fears being contaminated by congeniality.

As we approach, Beagle looks up. His eyes are heavy-lidded. His jowls sag over the tight collar of his uniform. "I want to talk to you alone, Major,'' he says.

Vanderslice fidgets. Waves vaguely toward the restaurant. "Okay. Sure. Well, I'll just go over here and get something to eat. You guys want anything?''

Beagle doesn't answer. Always the gentleman, Szabo shakes his head.

When Vanderslice is out of earshot, Beagle says, "Get us off this planet. Get us out of here now. We've been set up.''

We? Surprise makes my mind so blank it's like staring at a wall. Beagle's not in danger. I am.

"I've only gone over the preliminary reports,'' Beagle is saying. "But there's enough here to point to an attempted coup. The Tennyson government found out about it. They planted the bombs to kill the conspirators and cover up the revolution. Tennyson's designed to be a perfect world. And in a perfect world, Major, there can be no such thing as unrest . . .''

Beagle's eyes rivet to a point beyond my right shoulder. Vanderslice is walking toward us, carting a platter. He halts a few feet away. "You guys finished talking now? I brought snacks."

"All finished." I take a chair. Beagle's too smart—too *brilliant*—to be fooled by the obvious. "Beagle here was just telling me he's solved the case."

Blood drains from Szabo's cheeks so quickly it seems he'll faint.

I smile at Vanderslice. "Your government did it."

He puts the platter down in the center of the table and pulls up a chair. Apples. He brought us real apples cut in slices. And grapes like frosted green glass. A mound of cherries, still with their stems. Slices of melon too perfect, too orange to touch.

I pick up a cherry. Halfway to my mouth, my hand freezes. Beagle's glaring at me.

"It's there to find, Dr. Taylor." Vanderslice plucks a grape and rolls it between his fingers. "But wasn't finding it a little too easy?"

Of course it was. If Vanderslice found it, it had to be. And Beagle's so fucking *brilliant*.

Beagle's eyes never leave mine. "It's not good procedure to discuss this with a governmental representative present."

Vanderslice puts the grape on the table and regards it as if he expects it to talk. It lies there, separated from its peers: a pale-green enigma.

Beagle sits back. Laces his hands over his stomach. "Your orders called us here, Mr. Minister. You didn't go through Marvin. Do you really want us to solve this case, or do you need someone else to blame failure on?"

No one else seems hungry. I pop the cherry into my

mouth. A surprise: firmer than I had imagined; and sweeter. But an unexpected hardness inside.

Vanderslice says, "Marvin and I have divergent views."

"What about?"

"There was a man named Paulie Hendrix." A pucker between Vanderslice's eyebrows mars the blandness of his face. "He was killed in the fourth blast. The Warriors discovered incriminating statements in his DEEP, too. Marvin doesn't know who's behind the bombings, but he believes in revolutions. That's because he believes in sin, you see."

Vanderslice picks the grape from the table and squeezes it. He squeezes until the skin bulges. Until juice bleeds from its end. "When Paulie Hendrix died, Marvin stole his good name. His money. His house. He confiscated everything. Hendrix—" He stops himself as if startled by his own intensity. "Hendrix was always a little question-able. Not quite the ideal Tennysonian Christian. Marvin wouldn't hurt someone to protect himself, but he's always punished heresy. And there was lots of heresy in Paulie Hendrix's DEEP."

Vanderslice looks at me. At the grape. "Okay. He broke the Apostasy Laws. But there's a difference be-tween preaching evolution and fomenting rebellion. Paulie Hendrix would never be part of that."

Szabo takes an apple slice from the platter and bites into it. From the silence, a crisp, moist snap.

"How do you know for sure?" Beagle asks.

Vanderslice puts the grape on the table. He lays it down as if giving it rest. "Paulie Hendrix was my best friend."

8

I watch Vanderslice wend his way through the forest. Then Szabo blurts, "He lied."

Disappointment is painful, but I should have learned better by now. "What about?"

"I don't know. But he's lying to us."

"A shame," I say. And I mean it.

The sun through the skylights turns brassy. Day is dying in the lingering way of late spring. From the blue shadows of the lobby, peacocks call to each other in low oboe hoots.

"Still, though, I don't think he's dangerous." Szabo runs a hand fussily over his bald head.

Beagle says, "Don't let your personal feelings in the way."

"I'm a psychic. My personal feelings are supposed to get in the way. I don't have anything else to go on but personal feelings."

"Okay. Okay. But doesn't this seem too contrived? After all, the best way to keep an eye on us is to name a government insider as our liaison. Religion makes us uncomfortable, so to put us at ease, Vanderslice ridicules

Marvin. He doesn't know dick about us. He has no guar-
antee we won't tattle on him. If he was that stupid, how
long do you think he'd keep his job?''

The affable Szabo goes red-faced. Angry or pretending?
''Don't pull your M-8 status shit with me. I don't care
how famous you are. You may be a genius at statistics,
but I'm the psychic. Don't you try to tell me who to
trust.''

Szabo's overreaction is so incongruous that it had to be
planned. I understand now. Beagle and Szabo have already joined forces against me.

I get to my feet. ''Beagle? Find out all you can about
Paulie Hendrix. Get it to me by morning.'' The pair pretend to be startled wordless. ''I'm tired. I'm still recov-
ering from the Jump. Stay down here and fight this out if
you want.''

I walk through the darkening lobby through the lonely
cries of the peacocks. By the time the lift comes, the other
three have caught up. Arne is yawning.

In the silence of my room, I turn the Wall to a scene
of a summery meadow. The digitized flowers are so de-
tailed they look real. Lila, sunshine person and warm-
weather lover, would have liked it.

Still dressed, I stretch out on the bed. From the speakers
comes a querulous tu-wit, tu-wit and a whistle, as clear
as a piccolo.

*I'm at a beach. To my left is a scimitar of flat, amber
sand. To my right are mountains with dun-colored out-
croppings and dense purple shadows. It's a computer-
generated paint-by-number place.*

At the edge of the sand a young boy urinates into the #3 blue of the waves. Next to me, Lila says, "Oh look!" in a charmed touristy voice.

I'm embarrassed and uncomfortable. The beginnings of fear, like the start of a bad headache, pound at the base of my brain. "Don't look."

The boy pisses in an endless yellow stream. Lila, excited, is bouncing on her feet. "Look," she says.

I can't. Instead, I glance up the cliff and see, perched on the crumbling beige shale, a vast, decaying mansion. The building poises at the edge of doom like a deluded bird about to attempt disastrous flight. Its rococo facade is all curlicues and dark secret recesses, and there is something about the house that fills me with a hot, terrible dread; a cold, cramping pity.

"Look at me," Lila says.

I start to turn, realizing that turning is a mistake. But my head continues left as though destiny has given me a push.

"Look."

My head swivels notch by notch. I feel a scream burble up my throat. Anguish rushes into my mouth like a fountain.

I look—I look—oh God, I look down.

There are two red daisies in her palm.

"—oway?"

Wake with a gasp. The meadow is gone. A young dark-haired man's face fills the Wall. I can see every pore, every minute imperfection of his skin. That close, that huge, he's grotesque.

"Major Holloway?"

He's peering toward a spot past my left shoulder. I turn. Only blank wall to my back. The colonial has been polite enough to set the viewscreen to one-way.

My lips feel gummy. I slide them against each other. "Yes?"

The foot-wide eyes stare at the place where he assumes he'll find me. "There's been another explosion, sir. Minister Vanderslice wants to know if your team would like to come down. We have a programmed cab waiting at the front of the hotel for you."

Swinging my legs out of bed, I sit, shoulders hunched, head in my hands.

"Major?"

"Yes. Yes. Right away."

The man blinks out. The meadow returns. By the light of the Wall I dress, then walk down the corridor to Beagle's room.

Beagle answers my first knock. When I enter, I see his workstation is up and running.

"What time is it?" I ask.

Without hesitation, he answers, "Ten thirty p.m., Hebron time."

"There's been another bombing."

Beagle's room lights are on, but his Wall is set to a night scene of a lake. The moon rides high over the water. From the far shore a loon chuckles.

That's right. I was dreaming that Lila was with me. A boy was pissing in the ocean.

Pissing in the ocean, Lila said once. Fighting against Colonel Yi and the establishment is like pissing in the ocean. Can't you just pretend to agree with him and then do what you want? It's what I do with you.

"Don't you think we should go?" Beagle asks.

I jerk my head up. "What?"

"To the crime scene. Don't you think we should go?"

I nod. There was something in Lila's hand. Something . . .

"Will you wake the others, or should I?"

I scrub my hands over my face. "Let's both do it."

We wake Szabo from a sound sleep. Arne has been sitting up staring at a sunlit ocean with white-crested rollers and a pale golden crescent of a beach.

9

From the street it looks like any crime scene. A crowd, awed into quiet, clusters behind barricades. At the mouth of the subway tunnel God's Warriors compare notes like cops anywhere. Only the bright green of their uniforms makes them unique.

They look up as we approach. Cautious. Not knowing what to expect. I pass without speaking, and just inside the tunnel I take a breath. Prickly dust. And—yes, of course. I recognize it. Nothing smells more gummy, more cloying than blood.

I turn to the Warriors. "Who's in charge here?"

A cop with gold braid gives me a quick measuring look. "I am." He has a huge Alpine slope of a nose never touched by MedAltering.

"Get everyone out."

His eyes are an irate, molten brown. "We haven't finished searching for survivors."

"If we see any survivors we'll tell you. Now order your men to leave."

The team at my heels, I continue down the stairs, into a dingy fog of dust. Under the mobile floods Permacrete lies in chunks like the vertebrae of a huge Jurassic animal. Optic fiber nerves splay from the man-made bones.

A scattering of God's Warriors pick up their equipment and begin filing out. Arne doesn't wait for my orders. When I stop, he shoulders his analysis pack and continues down the stairs, Szabo behind him.

Beagle says, "Helluva deal. You're going to the store, maybe out to eat. Everything's fine, everything's safe. And the world ends."

The cavernous room below is the littered monochrome of disaster. This isn't the way murder is. Homicide is close-up and dirty. It leaves blood on the hands. It happens in dark, deserted alleys.

The subway had been a crowded, well-lighted place.

I tell him, "It isn't important if a bomb was used as the weapon. It's still murder." What happened doesn't look like murder. It looks like an upheaval of nature. "You feel sorrier for these people because they weren't killed by a knife? A garrote? Or doesn't that sort of thing happen up on M-8 level?"

Ceiling tiles don't fail on M-8. By day M-8s live deluged by sunlight. I wonder if it bothers Beagle that the subway riders of Hebron felt safe once, too.

"Don't lecture me, Major. I know crime."

"Oh, sorry. I forgot you wrote the fucking book on it."

Two passing Warriors eye me. One whispers something to the other. Too young for rank, so it doesn't matter. A backward glance, and they walk on.

When they're out of earshot, Beagle asks, "Do you want me down there? Or should I come with you?"

I don't want him with me. He'll listen to every question. Every word. "You've got infrared. I want you to double-check Arne's work." I turn and push my way up the stairs, past the Tennyson police.

At least thirty God's Warriors have gathered around the subway entrance. I find the cop with the nose and gold braid.

"I need to interview witnesses."

"Anyone left alive in there?"

"Now would be convenient."

He starts to say something, thinks better of it, and walks away. I follow him.

They've taken the witnesses to a building across the street. Seated, they line the halls. Their clothes are gray with dust. Their heads are lowered, their eyes empty. Catastrophe has made Earthers of them all.

I kneel beside a woman. "Ma'am?"

Unfocused eyes stray past the patch on my shoulder. "I lost my daughter," she says.

"I'm sorry to hear that. I need to—"

"She was right beside me."

"I'd like to ask you some questions . . . Ma'am? This is important, or I wouldn't bother you. I'm Major Holloway from the Home Force . . ."

The gaze sharpens. "You talk funny. Your uniform . . ."

Dull brown. But she's been dulled, too. A patina of dust coats her hair. "I'm from Earth."

She holds a piece of bloodied dress. Squeezing it, she looks away.

"Did you see anything, Ma'am? Before it happened? Did you see someone running away? Anything like that?"

The woman kneads the bit of dress with the mindless absorption of a cat. "I tried to run away. I grabbed at her. She was right beside me."

"I'm sorry to bother you at a time like this, but it would help if you could tell us anything out of the ordinary you might have seen."

The woman lifts her head. A groan comes from her throat, one so protracted that I think she'll run out of air and die there in the hall. In the dust. Among all those empty-eyed people.

Suddenly she gasps and makes the sound again. I scrabble to my feet. Is that how grief sounds? It's like a dumb animal, not human at all.

On the floor. There. By my feet. Right there. Two round drops of blood. An inch apart.

I catch my breath before the groan escapes. Hold it so long it's part of me.

"Really, Major . . ."

The Warriors' senior officer. I look up quickly. My expression must be fierce.

He backs away. "Ah, well. So. I think we have the situation under control. You can see we're interviewing the witnesses. No sense in going over the same ground twice."

God's Warriors are talking to the dazed. Death poisons the air. Every place I look I feel the pull of the scab over my own grief. I could tear my heart's wound open. Could bleed to death.

"Also we need to get some people down in the tunnel to take EPAT readings. Even if there aren't survivors, there are lots of dead still there. Relatives are waiting for news.''

My dream. Lila holding horror in the palm of her hand.

''Major?''

Don't look down. The red drops at my feet whisper, *Look. Look.*

''Major? Are you all right?''

''What?''

''If your stomach's queasy, we have some Nausease around here somewhere . . .''

''No.'' I clear my throat. ''You can talk to these people better than I can. I'll want everything, you understand?''

''Of cour—''

''Everything. And I want it downloaded to my net tonight.''

Before he can reply, I turn away. Head high, I walk past the survivors. By the time I reach the street, I'm nearly running. I shove through the Warriors at the entrance. Stumble down the stairs. The smell of blood glues itself to my nostrils. Dust makes me sneeze. When I reach Arne, I'm coughing.

''Have you found anything?''

Arne doesn't look up from his laser.

''I said, have you found anything?''

The demolitions man is so pale and insubstantial, he could have been assembled from the floating dust. Finally he turns. Unlike me, he remembered to bring all his equipment. The eyes over his mask are colorless. ''Goddamn it, Major! Get off my back! I won't know anything until I have the trajectory of the parakeet!''

Parakeet. He said ''parakeet.''

Across the cathedral-sized room Beagle stands near a chunk of metal, broad back to me. I can't tell whether he's frozen in horror or in thought.

As I pick my way through the rubble, I pass a slab of wall that has come down intact. A trickle of blood leads from one flat side. That body. I've seen jumpers, corpses turned to strawberry jam. But that body. Under there. Skin expanded with pressure, stretched to the breaking point. I look away.

When I walk up behind Beagle, he doesn't bother to turn. What seems inattention isn't. He recognized the sound of my steps long before I reached his side. A bit of robotic one-upmanship.

"Ground zero," Beagle says.

A boulder of ruddy metal sits on a marble base. A gold-leafed inscription reads: HAROLD AND MIMI TENNYSON AND TINKERBELL. GOD PROVIDED A WAY.

I recognize the remains of what once was a statue. On the lee side is a fold of bronze fabric, the sketchy outlines of an arm. A clawed avian foot rings an intact human forefinger. The bird is no place in sight.

"Tinkerbell. Was that a parakeet?"

Beagle's smile is whimsical. "Ah, you see, when Harold arrived, their good air/bad air counter was on the fritz. Couldn't tolerate the idea of turning around and going home. Didn't have the balls to try the air themselves. So over Mimi's squeaks of alarm, we must assume, Harold threw the parakeet out the ship's door, cage and all. Tinkerbell continued breathing. I like to imagine that it continued to squawk, 'I'm a pretty bird,' in its brainless parakeet way. Thus Tennyson colony."

I laugh. A wad of dust lodges in my throat. I sit on a broken piece of Permacrete to catch my breath. A whitish-blue hand is sticking out from under the rock. I get to my feet quickly.

"Why don't you call me by my name?" Beagle asks.

I step away from the rock. I'm careful not to look back. Murder should be intimate. Up close and personal. Victims should leave a mark on their killers.

"My name's Hoad. You may call me Dr. Taylor."

"Hoad Taylor's dead."

He fastidiously straightens the cuffs of his uniform. Like a murderer, there are smears of blood on his sleeve. A cautious man, but not careful where he puts his hands. "Did Colonel Yi tell you to call me that?"

The question brings me up short.

"Being named as your subordinate is obviously a demotion. An insult. A way to keep me in line. Was it Colonel Yi who asked you to call me 'Beagle'? Or did your instructions go higher?"

What happened between him and HF? "No. I thought of it."

He laughs. "I see. Is that your way of dehumanizing me? Do I intimidate you that much?"

"It's—that sad-eyed face. A hound's face." I can't really explain. What he reminds me most of is Toby, the dog in the Sherlock Holmes stories, even though that dog, as I remember, was a mixed breed. The first time I looked into Beagle's eyes I knew that he was a single-minded, predatorial thing. Yes, he intimidates me that much. Beagle is a mixed-breed Hound of Heaven.

He cocks an eyebrow. "You've just described a damned basset."

"Oh."

"I've decided to play along for now. But I can outsmart you. Remember that."

"You don't have to remind me. I know," I say.

I've surprised him. But why? "Well. You don't like the team very much. Is it because I'm not human and Szabo and Arne are gay?"

Impossible. They can't be gay. They would have never been allowed on the Tennyson team. Yi was so worried about sexual impropriety that he even excluded women.

"They were lovers once. Didn't you know?"

Absolutely impossible. Why is Beagle lying about this? "That wasn't in their files."

"Of course it was."

But I read the files carefully. There's no way I could have missed something like that.

A clatter. I look around. Sound in the huge hall is deceptive. From nearly fifty yards away I can hear the clicks of falling stones as Arne works his way through the rubble. The demolitions expert is whispering breathily to himself.

"Look what I found." Beagle takes a piece of bubbled black plastic from his pocket. "The bomb was in this, I think. Go ahead, Major. Arne's got all his measurements. Take it. There aren't any fingerprints to ruin."

From my right, a series of small taps. Arne has started a minor avalanche. Through the dark of the tunnel Szabo emerges. The psychic's bald head is streaked with dirt. He's remembered to bring his mask, but the dust must be bothering him. He wipes his eyes. The two meet in the ruins and converse in low tones.

I take the plastic. Turn it over and over in my hands. There's a sliver of copper wire embedded in it.

"We need to get Szabo out of here," Beagle says.

I look up. Szabo's crying. Arne has his arm around him.

I quickly give Beagle the bomb casing and pick my way through the debris. "Let's go. Right now. Get your hands off him, Arne."

Arne whirls. "Goddamn you! Can't you just leave him alone, you bureaucratic shit!"

I take a step backward, trip over a woman's gutted purse.

"What's the matter, Tommy?" Arne croons. "You can tell me."

Szabo can't speak for sobbing. Desperate to get air, he claws off his mask.

"Take him over to the side," I order. "It's the deaths. The deaths are bothering him, can't you see that?"

Arne doesn't move. Grabbing Szabo's sleeve, I lead him away. At a bench, I sit him down.

"You'll be all right in a minute." I look up at the others. "He'll be okay. I've seen this sort of thing before."

Szabo's sobs turn to exhausted gasps. "I'm sorry."

I tell him, "It's all right."

"It gets to me sometimes."

"Endwrapping."

He nods.

"Didn't HF know?"

A shrug. "I was getting better. I thought I had a handle on it. I thought—"

His voice rises. Gains a note of panic. Before he breaks down again, I shove the piece of plastic at him. "See what you can get."

He squeezes the burned bomb casing a moment. He kneads it the way the woman kneaded her daughter's dress. "Maybe I'm afraid to open up." Szabo looks at the bubbled black surface as if accusing it of treason.

"Nobody can blame you for that, Tommy," Arne murmurs. "Just put it down. It's okay."

"Butt out," I tell him. "And stay away from him from now on. Homosexuality is a crime here, or haven't you read your briefing report? Besides, there's no death on that bomb casing. Only murder. Let him do his job."

Arne tears off his mask. His thin face is drawn, his eyes are burning.

"Okay," Szabo says quickly. "I'm sorry, Major. Milos? The major's right. And I'll take the casing with me. I'll try later. I'll try harder. I'm not getting anything right now. Sometimes it happens. Psychometry isn't a science. Not like what Beagle does. Not like what Milos does."

The air in the subway tunnel stinks of dust and blood and smoke. Three hours since the explosion, and the rotten smell is starting. Szabo coughs. His eyes are wet. He wipes them.

"Well, if you're finished, let's leave. I'm choking in here. And I can see it's bothering you."

I don't expect an answer, but Szabo says, "Of course

it bothers me. That's the whole point. Every place I step has a horror story.''

''But not the right one.''

Szabo looks miserable. He puts the bomb casing down. ''No,'' he says. ''Not the right one.''

10

When we walk out into the moist sweet air of midnight, I find Vanderslice waiting. "Marvin's very upset," he says.

The God's Warrior with the large nose is standing next to Vanderslice. I wonder if they've been laughing at me.

"Stomach better now?" the Warrior asks me. "Still need that Nausease?"

Vanderslice turns and the cop's smile vanishes. "Lieutenant Stuven? It might be a good idea to send your men down into the tunnel and take those EPAT readings now."

The officer snaps to attention. In the harsh light of the floods I see the glisten of sweat across the man's forehead and down the long slope of his nose. "Yes, sir. Of course, sir. We would have been in there sooner, sir, if he hadn't—"

"I understand. Just get down there."

"Yes, sir. But you'll—"

Vanderslice's voice is so soft it chills me. "I'll explain to the Chosen, Danny. Get down there."

The cop pales. "Right away." He hurries toward his men.

Vanderslice shrugs. When he speaks again, his voice is casual. "Hope you don't mind, Major. I know it's late, but Marv wants to scream. It's best to let him yell."

"Beagle," I call.

He steps forward.

"You don't need sleep. Szabo and Arne can go back to the hotel. You come with me."

I'll need backup. I might need witnesses. Dangerous men never shout. They don't have to. I'm suspicious of Vanderslice's whisper and the way the cop blanched.

The limo is waiting. The interior smells of Vanderslice's spicy aftershave.

He doesn't offer us anything to drink. "What did you find?" he asks.

I look out the window at the sleeping town. "Nothing."

Vanderslice's eyes meet Beagle's. The construct stares back, poker-faced.

"Look. When we get to the mansion, let me do all the talking." Vanderslice leans toward Beagle. "And let's not remind him that you're a construct. He knows that, of course, but he conveniently forgets stuff. Marv's upset enough, understand?"

"No robot babble. I think I understand."

Vanderslice leans back and chews at a nail. The rest of the trip is silent.

On the third floor of the mansion we're met by a tight-lipped woman. Her eyes are wide with alarm. Wife? She's the right age. Or secretary? She's certainly frightened enough. Without a word, she opens the door to Marvin's office and ushers us in.

The Chosen of God is pacing the terra cotta tiles. In a

wing-backed chair a high-ranking God's Warrior nurses a drink.

As we enter, Marvin stops pacing. His face purples with rage. "God in Heaven!"

His shout is high-pitched and loud. The woman retreats, shutting the door behind her. The God's Warrior spills his drink and surreptitiously mops the upholstery with his sleeve.

"You were in there over an hour!" Marvin screams. "People were waiting for news! And do you have any idea what I had to tell them?"

Before Marvin can answer the question himself—because it appears that he is about to—I take a seat.

"That the Earthers had ordered my men out. And do you know what they said?"

Across the room Beagle considers his seating decision, then opts for a chair out of Marvin's line of sight.

"They said, 'But my father might be in there! My wife just went shopping and isn't home yet!' And do you know what my answer had to be? Do you have any idea?"

I lean back and regard my steepled hands.

"I don't know! I had to tell them I don't know! God help me! There were people crying on the phone!"

To my astonishment, Marvin halts his tirade to check his watch. "Nine forty-five the blast went off. It was after midnight when you finally decided to get out of there so we could finish listing the dead." Marvin has used up all stores of available anger. Now he stands depleted, his head down, his face weary. "I had to tell them we couldn't be sure there weren't more survivors bleeding to death in the rubble. One man was missing his wife and two children.''

"I'm sorry. There weren't any survivors. Didn't you think we'd check?''

The Chosen studies the ceiling. "You know what we are to Earth, Major Holloway? A dog on a leash. We can go just so far, and our master jerks us back. Sit up!'' he snaps.

I stiffen. But Marvin isn't looking my way. His gaze is riveted to the window and the sprinkling of blue-white lights beyond.

"Beg.'' In silken fury he adds, "Play dead.'' Marvin whirls. "Major. What did you find in there?''

"Nothing. Except by inference. The bombings are professional. Surgically neat acts of terrorism—''

"Neat? Surgically neat? That bloodbath? Blessed God, Major! You're talking in oxymorons. Nothing could be neat about it!''

Vanderslice, out of Marvin's peripheral vision, is motioning me to keep quiet. "I meant that whoever set the bombs off knew exactly what they were doing. That's what I meant. How are the God's Warriors trained?''

The Chosen's eyes turn glassy. His words emerge in a hiss. "Sweet Jesus. You're planning to blame this on me.''

"I'll investigate everything, but the government is the most obvious place to start.''

His fingers have started to tremble. "I ordered you to come. I can order you back.''

"If that's what you want.''

"If you can blame this on my administration, Earth can

take over Tennyson on an Article Five. And that's what you're planning to do. You'll take everything from us. Our sovereignty. Our wealth. Grasping little derelicts with your greedy little hands. You have an ugly world, Major. Ticks. That's what we call you. Did you know that? Ticks. And Earth is a crowded, scabrous hound. I want you out of here now. I want you off my planet.''

"Beagle." I rise. Beagle gets out of his chair.

"No!" Vanderslice is suddenly on his feet. "No. Listen. It's my fault, Marvin. I've made a mess of this investigation from the start. Let them stay and I'll resign.''

The glass falls from the God's Warrior's hand. Shatters like a bomb against the tiles. Beagle and I flinch. Vanderslice and Marvin stand, eyes locked. Marvin is breathing hard.

"There's no need—" Marvin begins.

"I can't solve this, Marv. Don't you understand? We're in a box, you see? A box. And Earth played fairer than I thought they would. Marv? Are you listening? Major Holloway caught Earth's most infamous criminal. He's been sent to colonies before, and he comes with their highest recommendation. Dr. Taylor—and I know how you feel about constructs, Marv. Believe me, I do—but there're only two others like him in existence. They spent a lot of money to preserve this man. Earth sent us their best. Don't order them home. Don't give Earth an excuse to step in. I know you're angry. I know that. But if you want a head to roll, Marv, make it mine.''

As if the offer has catastrophically aged him, Marvin shuffles toward the chair at his desk. He collapses into it and whispers, "Don't ask me to do this.''

"Marv?"

A lengthy silence. Marvin studies the floor. Then clears his throat. "Let them stay."

Vanderslice nods and motions us out. We walk past the wide-eyed woman, down the plush hall and through the marble entrance. When we climb into the limo, Vanderslice orders it to the hotel.

"Old Marvin." At my shoulder, Vanderslice sighs. "He can be excitable. I hope that—well, anything he said—I hope it hasn't offended you."

I don't bother to reply. I'm wondering what happened in that room. Szabo said Vanderslice is lying. But God, have I misjudged him? What could he be lying about?

"So," he asks, "what'd you come up with on Paulie?"

From the shadows of the opposite seat, Beagle says, "Paulie Hendrix, married to Talia Hendrix, and editor of *Godly Science*, a monthly journal. All the science that's holy we'll print, that sort of thing."

Vanderslice, as if he can hold it up no longer, drops his smile. "Right. What did you find out?"

All of Beagle I can see in the strobe of the passing streetlights is a sagging cheek. The downturn at one corner of his mouth. "He was into it up to his neck. According to his DEEP files he was tired of printing the acceptable, of being governed by the Apostasy Laws. He got sick of seeing good science ruined, and joined the revolution. Whether Marv decided to off him or not remains open to question, but that's the only question I have."

Vanderslice is shaking his head. "There's no revolution. It's all a smokescreen. I knew Paulie. He was a passive sort of guy. More at home with research. There's something else here. And you have to find out what." He looks at me. The entreaty in his eyes is naked. "Please, Major. You have to find out what."

"Beagle. Send the Hendrix files to my net."

A rustle. Beagle shifts his weight in the seat. "I'll send you a summary."

"I want the whole thing."

"Double work. Senseless. A time-waster."

I can feel the scrutiny of Vanderslice, his breathless anticipation. I take a deep breath. The air in the limo smells of aftershave. Of nervous sweat.

I wipe my hand down my face. It comes away greasy. "I want to see all of it. Maybe I'll find something you missed."

"I doubt that. I doubt that very much. Remember, I'm the expert here, not you. If there was a Hendrix pattern, I would have found it by now. I simply don't see the point."

"The point is," I say quietly, "that you're just a robot."

The sidewalk of the hotel is empty but for an automated luggage carrier. From the pine forest landscape lighting gleams. The gazebo seems to be sitting in a pool of moonlight.

When the limo drives off, Beagle doesn't move.

"Don't take the robot remark personally," I tell him.

Across the early morning air comes his hoarse bass. "Do you work at being a shit? Or has shittiness simply been thrust upon you?"

My laugh is inappropriate. Certainly impolitic.

"You need me, Major. Don't push me. Don't question my work like that."

"Look, I know you're M-8. I know your reputation. And I know there's nothing in the Hendrix files you missed. But you saw what happened between Vanderslice and Marvin. You may be smarter than I am, but I'm the better people-watcher. I'm trained that way. And when we're with off-worlders don't question my orders, you understand? They'll see a weakness in the team."

Beagle looks speculatively toward the hotel. "Sorry." A pause. "You're right."

The apology is a surprise. An unexpected peace offering. Since he's given in, I push him more. "What did you do to HF that makes you think they'll demote you?"

The famous Beagle as troublemaker? A construct as iconoclast? I doubt it.

He stiffens.

"I'm not the spy," I tell him. His face is held in such tight check that he looks more statue than man. I realize he doesn't believe me.

There's no point in arguing. I walk to a bench and sit. Beagle must not see the point, either. He sits at my side. "So what happened with Talia Hendrix?" I ask.

"She was banished out of bosom. She's living someplace on the south side now."

I stretch out my legs. Consider the tips of my boots. "South side. You know where?"

"Fifteen-forty Divine Mercy. Why?"

"Divine Mercy. Christ on a crutch. Where do they get these names? Did Vanderslice ever try to help her?"

Beagle shrugs. "Not that I can tell."

"If Hendrix was his best friend, why wouldn't he have helped his wife?"

"Maybe Talia Hendrix had become a political liability."

"Maybe. Is Vanderslice married?"

Beagle chuckles. "All the ministers have a wifey at home. It's expected with the job. Wifey's name is Jenny. Jenny and John. Has a precious sort of ring, don't you think? They have a one-year-old kid."

Did Lila ever want children? I don't know. We never discussed it. But she was realistic. The gardens on M-6 would have been enough. The flowers. The lighted walkways. And a small white dog.

From the pines an owl hoots. We both turn to look. Given Beagle's nightvision, it's probable he actually sees it.

The hoot sounds so lonely. "I wonder if they have mice. It would be pitiful to have owls and not have any mice."

Beagle, bored with the owl, swivels back. "Our boy Vanderslice may not have gotten along with Talia. That's possible." He gets to his feet. "Shouldn't we go in? It's probably getting cold for you out here."

Only then do I notice the chill. "Something in this Paulie Hendrix story doesn't fit, and Talia Hendrix has the missing puzzle piece. Maybe Vanderslice wanted her to disappear. Or maybe the south side's not as bad as the briefing reports say. I'd better take a cab to Divine Mercy."

"Isn't it a little late in the evening for that?"

I look toward the cabcall. Between the front of the hotel and the corner the sidewalk is dark. Why did I tell Beagle I would go? How could I trap myself like this? Now I'll have to walk through the shadows. I'll have to get in the cab alone.

I rise. Take a few self-assured steps before fear lames me.

"Hey!"

My terror is a room-sized weight I carry on my back. There are times it crushes me. Mornings I'm too tired to pick it up. At Beagle's call I turn.

"Sure you don't want me with you?"

If he goes with me, he'll see how my hands shake. How I jump at every noise. "No."

"Major? I'm not the spy, either."

I don't believe him.

12

The north side of the capital city dwindles into the south, growing darker with each block. There's no line of demarcation, no border guards, but the cab brings me into another country.

The sidewalks are narrow and cracked. No lawns, no single-family houses here, only looming monolithic apartments. The streets wear a coating of grime.

It's familiar, this place. Like the M-1 and M-2 Levels I work. Here and there are dark alleys and shadowed nooks: corpse-stowing places.

The cab stops on Divine Mercy. I tell it to stay, to keep its lights on. The door to Talia Hendrix's building is cheap Mockwood so scratched the grain's disappeared.

There's no answer to my buzz. Pulling up the collar of my jacket, I look around. Dim street lamps on each corner. A solitary lighted window beckons from halfway down the block.

"Orders?" the cab asks.

"Follow," I tell it.

Its headlights brighten the shattered sidewalk. It tags at my heels until I stop in the window's glow.

The window is smudged. I peer through a fog of grime. A tiny restaurant. No tables. No chairs. The counter is deserted. The door's open.

"Orders?" the cab asks.

"You can go."

I watch it speed away, taking most of the light with it. Then I walk in the door. The barkeep gives me a hostile glare.

"Coffee."

Wordless, she serves me. She slops the coffee over the top of the cup until it pools on the counter. I take a sip. The coffee's watery. Bitter. Just the way it tastes at home.

The south side of Hebron is like an Earth magstation— a place where people pass through and occasionally die. I study the barkeep. Was she born here? Or banished here years ago—long enough for her to get the dreary expression right? "You know a Talia Hendrix?"

The woman doesn't look up, but she pauses in wiping a glass. "Don't know nobody."

Her rudeness cheers me, like a familiar song cheers me when I'm far from home. "She's not in any trouble. I'm with Earth's Home Force. I just want to ask Mrs. Hendrix a few questions about her husband."

"Don't know nobody." She goes back to her wiping.

The door opens, letting in the damp breeze. A man shuffles inside. He bellies up to the bar. There's a cozy quality about this place: three people in a small room and no one talks. I drink in the seediness of it: the smell of old grease; the dirt caked in the corners. I look for roaches, but don't find them.

The man ruins the spell. He stares into my averted face. "Tick, ain'tcha?"

His breath stinks of alcohol and rotting teeth. Familiar sins. I look into my cup.

"Hey, you. Hey, Tick. Listen. She got some Hap-Assy back there behind the bar. Let's have a drink."

I stir the lukewarm coffee with a finger. "You know a Talia Hendrix?"

The drunk coughs. "I might. You could buy me some Hap-Assy."

A drink for old time's sake. I motion to the barkeep. She pulls an unlabeled bottle from under the counter and pours a shot glass. The drunk downs it. "Tick, huh? I been to Earth once."

"Do you know Mrs. Hendrix?" It doesn't matter if he does or not. I could sit here all night nursing my coffee. I could sit here until the sun drives back the dark.

The man rolls his eyes. "Coming through . . . coming through . . . No. It just ain't clear yet."

I laugh. "Give him the bottle." I toss her my card. She stares at its blank gold face, runs it through a rusting machine, and blinks when she reads the credit limit. Then she puts the card on the bar near my hand and sets the bottle near the drunk.

"You don't believe me I went to Earth, do ya?"

The man's a cheap wrinkled face over a cheap wrinkled suit. A hundred times I've come across his body lying in the streets. I don't mind. There's no blood. Their faces are always peaceful, as if they're asleep. Willing victims of habit.

"Sure I do." His eyes are sunken. His cheeks are a

jaundiced yellow-gray. Even if he quits drinking, he won't last long. "Have another drink," I tell him, because there are worse ways to die.

He pours a shot glass. Gulps it down. "Walked right through that door and seen Earth. Damndest thing I ever seen. Bright there, ain't it?"

"Where?"

"Earth. Awful bright."

"Yes, you know, it certainly is."

"Tal Hendrix." The man casts his eyes heavenward as if the answer is written on the ceiling. "Works night shift at the Meat Market on God's Gift."

He's surprised me. I didn't expect, I didn't need, any payment. Odd that his company was enough. "Oh? What time does she get off?"

"Four o'clock."

I check the time. Three-forty.

"Show ya. Got it right here." He shoves a dirty hand to my face. There's an HF patch in it.

HF patch. Ragged edges. Green where stitching held and shirt didn't.

Olive green. The color of Colonial Security.

My question comes out fast and hard. "How the hell did you get that?"

"Tolja. Tolja I got it off that tick when I went to Earth. Oh, they tried to stop me, but always was a light one on my feet. Bagged this when he grabbed me."

"Let me see."

Before I can snatch it, the nail-bitten hand snaps shut. The drunk is staring in horror out the window.

On the other side of the street, in the faint glow of the

corner street lamp, Reece Wallace is standing. Even in
profile I can feel the chill of his eyes.

The drunk grabs his bottle. Darts for the back door.

I have to follow. But the stool holds me. Reece holds
me. Jesus. Now he's looking. Reece Wallace is looking.
And it's as if he can see straight through the grimed window. Straight through the shadows in the bar.

Suddenly Reece turns and ambles into the dark.

My heart, my stomach, clench. "You see him? You see
that man?"

The barkeep shoots me a look.

"Out there. Out the window. Just a second ago. Didn't
you see that man?"

She lowers her head. Wipes the counter.

I dash out the front door. Coming around the corner is
a lone popcorn seller. Other than the vendor and her cart,
the street is empty.

I sprint to her. "You see that man?" She's hardly out
of her teens. A girl with a fresh-faced look—the kind
Reece liked to tie up and then carve on.

"What man?"

"The tall man in the black coat. Auburn sort of hair.
He was right there just a second ago. Right there. He
walked down this way. You couldn't have missed him."

"Oh. Him? Yeah, I seen him. You want Z-Tabs? Or
some Light-Up? Good Light-Up. Three-fifty a snort."

It's hard all of a sudden for me to catch my breath.
"No."

"Hey, mister. You okay?"

The street seems cramped and the girl fragile, as though
the dingy apartment walls are waiting to crush her. "Lis-

ten. You need to be careful. That man . . . that man's dangerous.''

Lock your doors, I want to shout as I once shouted too late at Reece's victims. Lock your doors, bar your windows and if you hear a knock, for God's sake, don't open up.

''You know him?'' she asks. I've spooked her. The girl is hurriedly shutting the hidden dope drawer, tossing the cold popcorn away.

The street where Reece has disappeared is dark. Too dark for me to follow. Tears of frustration sting my eyes. ''I killed him once,'' I say.

13

Proof.

There's no proof: no snap of Reece and his lopsided grin; no fifth HF patch on a planet where there should be four. My evidence darted out the back door; sauntered into the anonymous south side darkness.

It couldn't be Reece. Just someone who looks remarkably like him. I arrested him, didn't I? And testified against him. And nine months later watched him die.

I wanted his knees to go weak when they led him to the chamber. I wanted him to cry out. But they strapped him in and put the patches on his arm and a quiet minute later he closed his eyes.

Unfair that he died so easy.

It wasn't required, but I stood witness to Reece's autopsy. Just for the enjoyment, I watched his body burn. Six people attended the cremation. Me and the four members of my investigative team came roaring, back-slapping drunk. We watched his mother cry.

Down the narrow dark street moisture halos the street lamp. The cold seeps through my jacket and I shiver. I walk back to the restaurant. The light in the window is out. The door's locked.

I shout for the barkeep. Beat my fist against the metal. Cup my hands around my eyes, and peer through the glass. I pound on the door until my knuckles throb. No one comes.

I stand back in disbelief. I'm alone on the sidewalk. In the dark.

I step off the curb and stride quickly into the damp street. By the time I reach the corner I'm nearly running. I turn right. The street sign reads: Deliverance. Faceless apartment buildings. Sooty clones of each other. They shoulder up to both sides of the road.

Like M-1 Level. Only the ceiling's too high. Stars above. Faint pinpricks. Looking at them makes me dizzy.

I slow to a steady, determined pace. The pace of someone who has brightly-lit places to go. Friends to see. Any faster, and I'll draw attention. Any slower, someone
Reece
will catch me. My boots click against broken pavement. I listen for a telltale double tap of someone
Reece
following.

At the next corner I halt. My breath comes in hard-fought whoops. I fling out my hand. Brace myself against a building to keep from falling down.

Lila. Had she been frightened like this? Had she heard footfalls behind her? And if she turned, what did she see? Something so bad that for a moment she must not have believed it.

Kanz coming into my office. Face somber. Footsteps soft. Hands folded. *Dyle?*

I actually laughed. It couldn't be. Not Lila. She's too smart for that. Joking, because Kanz was so sad he scared me. *You guys fucked up.*

A cluster of cops at the mouth of a dark alley. Warning me back. Me with the smile on my face. Not Lila. She wouldn't be stupid enough to go in there. Never careless enough to be a victim. The DNA match is wrong. It's wrong. Sometimes that happens. You know that.

Walking forward. Tap of boots on pavement. Kanz at my elbow, his voice dangerously soft.

Don't look.

My knees didn't soften. I didn't cry out. With shock, incredulity always falls like a blanket. It's the only proof I have of God.

My shoulders convulse. I try to take a breath, but my chest heaves. No air comes in. I can't tell if the sound that emerges is sob or gasp. Lila. She lived long enough for even the divinity of cognitive dissonance to lose patience.

Gradually the spasms stop. The noises in my throat fall silent. I wipe my eyes, then raise my head.

The street sign above me reads: God's Gift.

Steps cautious, I round the corner. Down the street is a lighted sign: MEAT MARKET. A man is standing in its glow, staring my way. Not Reece. Not whipcord thin. Not a man who would be quietly deadly. He's burly as Beagle. The arms crossed over his chest have aged to muscle and flab. He has a butcher's apron and huge bone-cracking hands.

He's still watching me. There's at least half a block between us, too much of a distance for me to read his expression.

I check the time: 3:52.

I step off the curb, cross the street, and walk toward the light.

"Evening," the man says.

"I'm looking for a Talia Hendrix."

He jerks his head toward the door. "Number Three."

A glance over my shoulder, but he's looking at the street again. Not coming after me. I enter the building. The inside is starkly lit. The corridor's clean and unpeopled. I open the third door down, and tense as it shuts fast behind me.

The tiny room is blinding: white floors; white walls; white ceiling. It's empty.

"Hello?"

A muffled woman's voice. "Hello."

Behind me, near the door, is a card scanner. In one corner a video eye the size of a hen's egg. I look into it. "I'd like to talk to you."

"No talking. Find you a slot and put it in."

The woman's voice comes from behind the left-hand wall. Its thin, pliable surface is marred by thumb-sized puckers. I take my card from my pocket and push it through.

"Are you kidding? Jesus. Just a minute."

A flurry of muttering, shuffling activity. The camera lens swings toward me and locks.

"Tick," the woman says. "No wonder."

"Can I see you? Can you come out from behind there?"

"We don't do it that way. And you pay when you leave. Just find one of the slots comfortable for you and stick it through. The door behind you is locked. When you're finished, put your card in the reader, and the door will open."

Talia Hendrix sounds as if she's on the down side of forty. "I don't understand."

"Christ." Her mutter is so quiet I can barely hear it through the rubberized wall. "A blow job, okay? That's what we do here: blow jobs. No fondling, no kissing. Just a blow job."

Surprise makes me laugh. "Okay. We have a misunderstanding here, I think. I was looking for the Talia Hendrix who was married to Dr. Paulie Hendrix. I need to talk to her about her husband's death."

A long, weighty silence while the laughter dies in my throat. It's a furtive silence, somehow a sad one, one in which the bright white room holds its breath.

"I'm that Tal Hendrix." Her voice sounds older now, more like a tired fifty. "I get off work in about ten minutes. Wait for me in the hall."

—————— 14 ——————

While I wait, a man walks in. He gives me a furtive look. Baby face, neat hair, nice clothes. Too well-groomed for the south side. And then I recognize him. One of the God's Warriors at the bombing. One of the junior officers who passed me on the stairs.

He recognizes me, too. Lowering his head, he walks faster. I tense as he approaches the third door. Relax as he passes by. At the fourth he enters. The door slides shut. A light over the jamb changes from green to amber. For occupied.

I check the time. 3:59. I study the green light above Mrs. Hendrix's door. At 4:08, I return to the room.

Behind me a hiss as the door shuts. "Mrs. Hendrix?"

No answer.

Louder. "Mrs. Hendrix?"

"Off duty." A different voice. Younger. Early twenties. Maybe even teens.

"Is she still here?" What if there's a back door? Of course. There has to be. This sort of place, there's always a back way out.

A pause. "Sir. I can't tell you that. We're not allowed

to fraternize with the customers when we're off duty.''

"I'm a police officer."

The camera swings my way. A confused, "I'm sorry, but—"

I jerk my head up, face the camera. "I'm a police officer with Earth Home Force. I need to talk to Mrs. Hendrix. I need to talk with her now."

"I can't—"

"You're impeding a murder investigation. Where is she?"

"I—" Scared. A young girl torn between the rules of her job and the cold threat of the law.

"Where!"

"She went home. She—"

Ran out on me. While I was waiting for her in the hall, she ran out on me. I slam my card into the scanner. Sprint for the door. The street is empty but for the guard. I hunch my shoulders against the chill and stride toward Deliverance, moving fast.

Wait. A block down God's Gift. Something dark in the shadows. No. Imagination. But then, through the spotlight of the street lamp comes the sway of a red coat. A glint of gold hair. A proud, tilted head.

An instant's strobe of color, and she's gone.

My heart stops. My throat closes on her name. I run through the street lamp's island of safety. Toward the next corner. The next lamp has failed.

Dark here. So black that my vision swims. Not this. Not now. I want to go back to the Meat Market. There're lights there. I'll call a cab. I'll . . .

My whole life.

Reece and now . . . But what if? What if you could roll back time? When I was a kid, I fantasized about it. In my bed. In the dark. Didn't use to be afraid. Only lately. Only after.

But what if I could go back? My whole life. Stop it this time. And what if all I had to do is walk through the dark? It's the walk, I told Kanz. My wife walks like an M-9. A proud walk. It throws murderers off stride.

What if someone's waiting for her? A knife. The alleyway. But I can't walk proud like that. I blunder through the dense black where she disappeared. Buckled sidewalk trips me. A double tap. My own echo. I'm not sure which direction I'm going until I turn the corner.

Garish kiosk—the only spot of color on Revelation. A blond woman in a red coat stands there. Back to me. Oh. Back to me. Reading the menu.

I have to hold my breath. Careful. Careful. Does she hear my heart pound? Frighten her. Lose her. Not again.

She whirls. Her eyes are wide. And brown. Her eyes are brown. Her nose is wrong. Her mouth too wide. Not Lila. What's the matter with me? Of course not Lila. Not Reece.

But something in the way she holds her head. Something in the way she walks. From a distance . . .

"Oh," she says dismissively. "It's you."

I swallow hard.

She turns her back on me again. "I thought you'd take the hint."

"Mrs. Hendrix?"

Her shoulders tense. She passes her card through the reader. Punches her order up.

"I just want to talk to you."

Hold you.

I walk to her side. Under the coat, her body's not at all like Lila's. Stockier. Thicker waist. Larger breasts.

She sees me looking. "Nothing personal, but if you want to talk about Paulie, let's keep it business."

"Yes." I cough into my hand. My cheeks burn. "All right."

She takes a sandwich from the food slot. A cup of coffee from Beverages. Then she selects a table and finds a chair.

I order my own coffee. "Why did you run?" I keep my back to her. To that blond hair. Tilted chin.

"It's easier that way."

No. No, it's not. "Is it?"

"You think Paulie's innocent."

An electric jolt of shock. When I pick up my coffee, my hand shakes. "I'm exploring that possibility." I take a deep breath and turn. Not so hard to do. Not so much like her. I carry my coffee to the table and sit down. "How did you guess that?"

"Deduction." Mrs. Hendrix has a smile that makes her look like a schoolgirl. "If you thought Paulie was guilty, there'd be no reason to hunt for me in the south side, a quest that I'm sure was not without either its frustrations or dangers."

A smart woman. Too smart? Is that why Vanderslice never helped her? "Was your husband involved in a revolution?"

"He was involved in rebellion up to his neck." Her smile widens. Her eyes fill with devilment. "Paulie was motivated to see the Tennyson government fall. So was I. We worked for years at it." Her gaze shifts. She looks across the empty dark street. "Perhaps 'rebellion' is too strong a word. It was no secret how either one of us felt. Paulie skirted the limits of the Apostasy Laws. In private, he broke them. But no one ever knew. It was never a crime to complain about the government. Everyone just considered it outré."

"What about the plans found in his DEEP?"

Her eyes lock with mine. Not a kind brown. Nor a warm brown. Resilient. Like hardwood. "And therein lies the conundrum. Paulie never had anything in his DEEP."

"How can you be so sure?"

"Paulie was a brilliant man, but he was uncomfortable with programming. All his computer commands were verbal. He had no idea how to create a DEEP. There's only one way that information could have got there: it was planted."

The kiosk's icemaker hums and then upchucks a clattering load of ice into its steel bin. I look at the dented machinery and the red and blue sign above: DANGER. INJURY MAY RESULT FROM NON-PAYMENT.

"I've been told that nobody can access a DEEP except from the home port."

"That's what they want us to think. Don't be naive, Major."

She's looking at my insignia. I remember the HF patch in the drunk's hand. A captain. The drunk tore the patch from a Colonial Security captain. Where had the drunk found the money to travel to Earth? How could he have taken that patch through the Jump without somebody questioning him about it?

I ask, "Are you a programmer? What makes you think an outside agency got into his DEEP?"

"I know because I know what was in there."

"You want me to believe that when the God's Warriors searched your house one of them planted that evidence."

"I don't want you to believe anything."

Mrs. Hendrix finishes her coffee and begins tearing flower-petal strips down the cup. She must not have been hungry. Or memory has upset her. Did she love him? The sandwich lies untouched.

I'm suddenly furious with Vanderslice. How could he forget her? How could he leave her to this? Her head is tilted now, but tilted down. She looks so sad, I think. "Mrs. Hendrix," I say gently. "After the bombing, who was in your sperm?"

Her expression freezes. I feel my own sag. The word hangs in the air between us. "I'm sorry," I whisper. "Sorry." I clear my throat. "Did anyone ever come into your home?"

She laughs. She has a merry, gut-loud laugh. A woman's version of Szabo's. "What a delightful Freudian slip. God, Major. Don't look at me like that. We use a heating coil, lubricant and Smart Plastic. I put the device over the man and let it go. Oral sex is a misdemeanor here. The average Tennysonian male has no idea how it feels. The only customer who's ever seen through the ruse was a miner from Jones' Paradise. Although I have no doubt you would have caught on quickly. My job bothers you for some reason, doesn't it? Odd. Your being from Earth. Being a cop.''

She wants me to laugh with her. I don't. What she's told me should make me feel better. Why doesn't it? ''Mrs. Hendrix, please: Did anyone ever get in your house?''

''They wouldn't have to. Whatever anyone wants you to believe, you *can* access DEEP files through the net. But the only people with that type of programming sophistication are in the Tennyson government.''

Four forty-five and morning is coming on. The sky, the street, turn milky gray. Buildings emerge from the shadows. The kiosk, with a trickling sound and rich warm scent, begins perking a new batch of coffee.

I close my eyes.

''You're tired,'' she says.

I open them again. Color from the kiosk's sign bleeds on the street. I yawn. ''Just a little.'' My eyelids droop. But that's all right. It's all right to be sleepy. Everything's safe now. I sit and watch morning chase the shadows. ''John Vanderslice. How close was he to your husband?''

''Oh, yes. John.'' Her face is droll. ''When Paulie was younger they were friends. John was Paulie's student, you know. Then things changed. They drifted apart.''

''Vanderslice is convinced that your husband is innocent.''

Strong emotion pulls her lips down. I wonder if it's fury or grief. ''He should know.''

''You mean they kept in touch?''

''I mean that if anyone could get into Paulie's DEEP

files and put something there, it had to have been John Vanderslice.''

''It was Vanderslice who told me DEEPs are inaccessible.''

''Well, disinformation *is* his job.''

The sky above is pearl. Pinkish gray at the horizon. Tennyson's sun hangs in wait just below the terminator.

''But I thought Vanderslice was the Minister of Science.''

''Yes. The Science Ministry controls surveillance,'' Mrs. Hendrix says.

''I'm sorry? I don't understand.''

She laughs. A bitter one this time. ''John Vanderslice is head of the secret police.''

——— 15 ———

No cab calls on the south side. That's what she tells me. I don't want to leave her, but I take off at a run. Four blocks. Easier now. Five. Just a memory. Until a stitch in my side slows me down.

Through gaps in the buildings I catch a glimpse of a red sun peeking over the horizon. Light turns the streets apricot and gold. Seven blocks.

Vanderslice. That bastard. I should have known. Too easygoing, too affable. And what does he have on Marvin? Damn. What does he know about me?

My steps become a painful hobble. There's a burning ache in the back of my legs. How many blocks now? I've lost count.

The buildings here are smaller. Nice eight-plexes and four-plexes. Some trees. Around the next corner I come across a man lurking near a clump of bushes.

He hears my approach and turns. Young. Expensive suit. Expensive haircut. Expensive briefcase. He reminds me of Vanderslice.

"Where's the nearest cab call?" I ask.

He backs up, not as if I frighten him, but as though

he's afraid of getting dirty. "Excuse me?"

"A cab call. Where's the nearest cab call?"

"Four blocks west."

"Four blocks?" I'll never make it. "Goddamn!"

His guileless face tightens. Not used to the language. Not used to the anger.

I ask, "What are you doing out here?" He's on his way to the office. He'd have a clean office. With a window.

Not used to being talked to like this. "What are you doing out here?"

"I'm with Earth HF."

He doesn't understand.

Of course not. Ticks. To them we're ticks. "I'm a police officer, and I just asked you a question. What are you doing out here?" If I had my weapon, I'd shove it under that clean-shaven chin just to wipe the superciliousness from his face.

"I'm waiting for a friend to pick—"

"Good. I need a ride downtown."

Cautiously: "Oh. Downtown? We're going, uh . . . I don't think we're going that direction. Sorry."

He's lying. And there's nothing I can do about it. Nothing I can do about Vanderslice. Nothing. I lean close, face-to-face. "Fuck you." Enough fricative in the word to mist him with spittle.

His smile drops. When I walk away, his shocked gaze tracks me, and it feels good.

Four blocks west, near the cab call, a woman is kneeling before a flower bed. Why is she weeding? Doesn't she have a bot to do that for her? In the air, the heady scent of moist loam.

She stops working. When I catch her eye she hurriedly looks away. Not frightened, but . . . what? Then I recognize that look. She's not afraid for her life. She thinks I'm going to ask for money.

I run my hand over my cheeks and feel the stubble. My eyes feel gritty and swollen. I probably stink. A cab's waiting. I climb in and order it to the hotel. By the time I reach the Hebron Crossroads it's already nine o'clock.

I walk past a curious desk clerk and take the lift to the eighth floor. Beagle doesn't answer my knock. Szabo and Arne don't either.

I've arrived too late. Vanderslice has picked them up.

Wary, I walk to my own door, key in my hand. Someone's probably waiting inside. A group of God's Warriors. Smiling, because they won't want to alarm me. They'll have on immaculate uniforms. They'll be clean-shaven—not a hair out of place. They'll smell of after-shave and they'll be pleasant. So polite. Sorry to bother you, Major.

There's no other choice. No place to hide. I slide my key in the slot and open the door. The room's empty. The Wall is blinking a non-emergency green-over-black message: ROOM 810.

My vision blurs. I look at the message again, hoping that I'll understand it. Finally I sigh and walk down the hall.

Szabo opens the door to 810. There's a half-eaten donut in his hand. "Oh. Major. We were worried about you."

I push past him, into a huge three-room suite. Arne sits

at a table, drinking coffee and contemplating a Sheet. Beagle is crouched over his workstation.

"Beagle! What the hell do you think you're doing?" I can hear the sound of my own voice. Too sharp. Too loud.

"Did you order this? Did you?" I would have arranged for a work suite if I'd had the time. Why didn't Beagle just give me the time?

"Goddamn it! I'll make the decisions around here. I don't give a running fuck how famous you are. Or how goddamned smart you are, either. I was made team leader. If you have a problem with that, tell me. If you want to requisition something, you go through me. Do you understand?"

"Yes." His gray eyes are as level, as emotionless, as his voice. "Yes. Thank you, Major. I quite understand."

"Good." I turn. Szabo and Arne are staring. "Szabo. Get on the net. Find us a house. Do it now. I want an isolated place. And then I want everybody to pack. I want us out of here." The words spill from my lips. Before I know it, I've said too much. The room is probably bugged.

"Major? What's wrong?" Beagle asks.

I snatch the Sheet from the table and write: VANDERSLICE IS HEAD OF THE SECRET POLICE.

Beagle rises. Takes the Sheet. He looks at the message and nods. No surprise in his expression. He suspected. Of course. He's so fucking brilliant.

"What?" Szabo is asking. "What's going on here?"

Beagle hands him the Sheet and Szabo, reading, pales. He puts the Sheet down and goes quietly to his own workstation.

I tell Beagle, "I'm going to read the Hendrix files."

Not waiting for his protest, I go to his station and scroll. Issues of *Godly Science*. Editorials by Paulie Hendrix condemning Vanderslice for pandering to Marvin, for stupidity, for bad and incompetent science. Hendrix and Vanderslice weren't best friends. They must have hated each other.

So Beagle knew what Vanderslice was lying about. How long was he going to keep the information to himself? M-8. Thinks he's better than me. Thinks he can sucker me like Vanderslice has.

I raise my head, then notice the tension in the room. Everyone is pointedly ignoring me. Arne has his head lowered. Szabo is letting his station do the search. From a pile of debris he picks a brown wallet and turns it over and over in his hands. What message is he getting from it? There's an unSzaboish glower on his bearded face.

They're all annoyed. What were they talking about before I got here?

Beagle picks up the Sheet from the table and writes: VANDERSLICE PLANS TO KILL MARVIN.

How does he know that? Did Vanderslice tell him?

HE WANTS TO BE CHOSEN OF GOD. SOMETIME SOON NOW, MARV WILL DIE IN A BOMB BLAST.

Oh. Yes. I understand. Clever. Hiding one murder in a forest of others. My eyes shift to Beagle's brown sleeve and I remember the HF patch. The olive green cloth.

I tear the Sheet from him and scrawl: COLONIAL SECURITY'S HERE.

Finally some expression. A flicker of alarm passes over Beagle's jowled face.

I write: FIND OUT IF THE EXPLOSIVE MATERIAL COMES FROM TENNYSON OR EARTH. I climb to my feet. Give the Sheet to Arne. He flings it angrily back and the metal sheath hits my chest hard. I'm too surprised to react.

"I'm getting sick and tired of your overbearing crap! Don't think I haven't figured it out, Major. You're reporting on everything I do, and you're sending it to that dyke bitch Hiko Black. Don't treat me like I'm stupid."

A dark shape zips past me and smacks the wall. Szabo is on his feet. Lying against the opposite wall is the wallet.

"Goddamn it!" Szabo screams. "Stop it! Will you all just shut up!"

Arne's lips purse. "Holloway's a spy. That jealous bitch is after me. Busted me to M-3 just because I'm better than her."

What is he talking about?

"Jesus Christ, Milos." Szabo's voice is ugly. It doesn't sound like him at all. "Grow up. You're not the center of the goddamned universe!"

Arne is surprised. Confused. Maybe hurt. Oh. I see it now. Definitely hurt. "I wasn't the one who moved back to Level 4. You couldn't take it. Couldn't give me a chance. Didn't believe in me enough to—"

"Believe in you? M-4 was as high as you're ever going to get. It's that attitude of yours. That's what busted you. What drove me crazy. How do you think it felt coming home day after day, listening to your crap?"

Arne's pallid skin has grown so pink that I have to drop my eyes.

Szabo lurches forward. He towers over the seated Arne.

"It was always, 'They're after me, Tommy,' 'They have something against me, Tommy.' If you cared, you would have kept your mouth shut. Maybe you would have noticed that I had problems, too. Well, I came to grips with what was bothering me, Milos, and I had to do it alone. I didn't leave because they busted you. Face it. I left because I couldn't stand living with you anymore."

A raw silence. Then Arne says, "Fuck you," in a tiny, tiny voice.

Szabo's anger is spent. He shakes his head. Walks toward the window and gazes out.

Louder, but not by much: "Fuck you." Tears swim in Arne's eyes. He lunges to his feet and slams out the door.

Beagle strolls over to Szabo's station. He says, "Um. The search stopped. Looks like we found us a house."

At the window, Szabo turns. "Sorry for losing my temper."

"Forget it," I tell him.

"No. It was unprofessional. I'm sorry."

"It happens. No problem. Forget it." I hope he'll shut up. It was me who was unprofessional. Accusing Beagle. Raising my voice.

"It was the endwrapping," Szabo says. "It still bothers me. You saw what happened at the bombing site. But for a while it was like I couldn't put the job down. Not ever. It was with me when I went to sleep. When I ate. I felt like it was on my hands and I couldn't wash it off."

Murder lingers in the mind—gummy as the smell of blood. Does Szabo think just because I'm not psychic I can ignore that?

I walk over to him. "Look. You don't have to explain.

Just start getting your stuff together. I want out of here."
I grab his arm.

He jerks away. "Don't touch me!"

Beagle looks up from the screen.

Szabo's blue eyes are wide. Frightened and angry all
at the same time. His voice is a terrifying whisper. "I can
feel your fear all the time, Major. It wakes me up at night.
I could sense it in the ship and it felt like you were
screaming. God. The only time I felt fear like that was
when I touched the hand of a schizophrenic."

A syllable of surprise drops from my mouth. I back up
so quickly I nearly trip over my own feet.

"No wonder HF wants me to keep an eye on you. I
see the reason for it now. You're the weak link. You'll
end up getting us all killed. You know that?"

Beagle says, "That's enough."

My God. Szabo's the spy. And HF thinks I'm crazy.

"You can't keep the team together." Szabo's cheeks,
his bald head, are crimson. "Shit. You can't even keep
yourself together."

Szabo. I never really thought it would be Szabo.

Beagle, too calmly: "That's enough, Szabo. You've
said enough."

But it has to be Beagle, too. They've planned this.
They've plotted against me.

"Beagle!" I can't look at either one of them. "Get your
goddamned suitcase packed. Szabo. Get the address of
that house. I want us out of this hotel in ten minutes."
And I hurry out the door without bothering to see if they
obey.

16

I'm packing when a change in the room's light makes me turn. Vanderslice is standing in my Wall. He's stopped at an outside pay phone. Behind him is a thicket of saplings. And in the distance, a park. Children are playing there.

His smile is charming and bewildered. "Why do you want to leave the hotel?"

The muscles in my back knot. High-pitched laughter from the receiver makes me flinch. Dots of color move across a green field: children chasing a ball.

"Major? I have good reason to suspect you're in danger."

Vanderslice is too hard to look at. I watch the park, instead. There's something else there, taller than the children. And still. Rounded shape. A rabbit. A bot rabbit with a waistcoat and top hat.

"You went to the south side last night and spoke to Paulie's widow." Vanderslice's face is friendly, but menace has crept into his tone. "Shouldn't have done that."

Did he have me followed? Did he question her? I try

to swallow, but my throat is tight. "Mrs. Hendrix? She's a close-mouthed bitch."

A smile. "Yes. You're absolutely right. That's the Tal I know."

"I didn't find out much."

Blood-curdling scream. So high and clear and sudden it makes me start. No. The children. Just playing. Did they beat Mrs. Hendrix? Do they interrogate that way?

His expression is chagrined. "Secret police. Sounds so sinister, doesn't it?"

The rabbit chases a shrieking child. All round body. All creamy pink fur. Sinister. Is she still alive?

"Okay." Vanderslice shrugs. "All right. So some of the God's Warriors go undercover. Undercover doesn't automatically mean bad. In fact, I keep a contingent around the hotel just to make sure you're safe. So you need to stay put. Unless I'm with you. If you go out alone, who knows what could happen?"

I force myself to relax. "How did you find out we're leaving? Did the net pick up on it? Are our rooms bugged? That's it, isn't it? Our rooms are bugged. I thought so. If you listen long enough we'll eventually tell you who the perp is." Laughingly now. Cop-to-cop. Does my voice shake? "Fuck you for a lazy bastard, Vanderslice. I'm not carrying you up the Glory Road on my shoulders."

"Okay. Fair enough. Together, all right? We'll work together. It's just that you were going to shut me out, Major. And I couldn't have that."

I return to my packing so he can't read terror in my face.

"I'll bet you've been reading old copies of *Godly Science*. That what happened, Major? And you must suspect me now. Look, if that's what this is about, I need to talk to you privately. I can be over there in ten minutes."

I can't turn around. Not even to look at the rabbit. Sinister. He'll see the fear in me. The pretense of indifference is so hard. "Don't bother. We'll be gone by then."

"Oh, come on. What's the matter with you? You're acting like I scare you to death."

I whirl. Face him. So difficult. "You lied to me. That pisses me off."

Vanderslice brings his wrist up fast and stares at the face of what I have assumed is a watch. Not a watch at all. That has to be a delayed-read voice stress analyzer. Now Vanderslice realizes I'm lying, too.

"What else did she tell you?" He isn't smiling anymore.

He killed her. God. I know he killed her. My fault. Mine. You'll get us all killed, Szabo told me.

But Vanderslice is the one who looks scared. I don't understand. "Wait a minute. Just . . . just stay there, Major. Please. Just stay there for fifteen minutes. I want to explain."

He severs the connection. Darkness swallows the children, the rabbit.

Fifteen minutes. I shove my suitcase closed and dart out the door. I'm out of breath when I reach Beagle's room. "Aren't you packed?"

"Yes. I was—"

"Let's go now. The place is rotten with undercover God's Warriors and Vanderslice is on his way."

Beagle's calm. Too calm. "Fine, Major. I understand. I won't be a minute."

He steps into his room. I run to Arne's door. To Szabo's.

"Let's go!"

By the time they emerge, Beagle is waiting with his suitcase. I check the time. Nearly time. Five minutes gone. Another minute lost waiting for the lift to come.

In the lobby, the hotel clerk tries to head us off. "Wait. You're leaving? You can't be leaving! Check-out time's past. But that's all right. I suppose that's all right. Please, sir. Management will want to know: Why are you leaving like this? Was something not to your satisfaction? Just tell us. The Hebron Crossroads always tries to make things right."

We stride out the door into the bright noon sun. No one but the hotel clerk makes a move to stop us.

"Your bags!" he says, dismayed. "You should have called a bot for the bags. We have bots for that!"

A bus is waiting in the circular drive. I climb into it and fling my suitcase into the overhead compartment. "Szabo. Give it the address."

Szabo sounds perplexed. "I don't understand what's happening here. Why you're so upset . . ."

"The address, damn it! Now!"

"Thirty-four sixteen Mount of Olives."

As the bus jerks forward, I look out the window. There's a group of shoppers walking to and fro on the other side of the street. Brightly dressed women. Bright as the children. And something taller. Something still.

"Stop!" I gasp. "Bus! Stop!"

The bus stands on its brakes.

I point, and Reece turns away. Just the back of his head now. Just the flash of his auburn hair in the sun. "That man!" I shout. "Don't you see that man?"

Reece trots into a nearby alley.

Beagle leaps off the bus and sprints for the opposite sidewalk. I run after. Beside me, cabs and cars screech to a stop. I push through a gaggle of onlookers. The entire planet of Tennyson seems to grind to a halt.

Ahead. The other end of the alley. A flash of brown as Beagle darts into sunlight and disappears around a corner. Feet pounding. Breath in whoops. I stagger around the edge of a building and run headlong into Beagle's back.

He whirls, his face contorted. "I lost him! Too many fucking people!"

We've stopped traffic here, too. In the open-air market a crowd of shoppers raise their heads at the profanity.

I can't catch my breath. Comets spark through my vision. Black flowers blossom like the onset of night.

"Major? You all right?"

"Tired."

He puts a steadying hand on my arm and I'm too exhausted to fling it off. "Rest a minute," he says. "Your pulse rate's through the roof."

"You saw him, then? You saw him?"

"I saw your reaction. Saw him run. He's good. Left a perfect infrared trail down the alley, but he knew where he was going. There's too much walk-friction here to single out his steps. You know him, don't you?"

I nod. Close my eyes. Sparklers, but fewer now.

"From Earth? The one from Colonial Security?"

I don't understand why I say it. Don't understand how I can be so sure. "He's the HFCS captain."

"The planet of Tennyson was founded over one hundred and fifty years ago by Harold and Mimi Tennyson of Earth . . ."

I open my eyes. A girl in a frilly blue dress is leaning toward me.

"What's the holo for?" Beagle asks.

I can't help laughing. When I laugh, I cough. "She's saving your soul. And Marvin's not even sure you have one. Tell her you're not interested and she'll go away."

Beagle tries, but the girl ignores him.

". . . a place where they would be free . . ."

She knows. She recognizes Beagle as a robot. "Get out of here," I tell her and she vanishes. "Beagle? I saw a holo like that the other morning. They approach humans without EPATs. Churches are meticulous about visitor records. What if . . ."

Beagle's face lights up. "The HFCS guy wouldn't have an EPAT. Jesus fucking Christ! We can nail him!" He's still smiling when a God's Warrior walks up and writes him a ticket for public profanity.

17

It's a slow walk back. On the broad avenue car radars see us coming and have time for leisurely stops. I look through the windshields. The Tennysonians aren't hostile to our jaywalking. They're polite. They're patient. They're so damned bored.

On the island that separates the eastbound from westbound lanes, I stop.

"Still tired?" Beagle asks.

"Just a minute." I lean over and prop my hands on my thighs.

He couldn't be Reece. Still, I know why he wears that face. MedAltered. HF can't control me, so they want to break me down. A little reminder: You're not that smart. Not as smart as you think.

Trouble-maker.

Iconoclast.

They wouldn't promote me, but I was too successful to bust. Not like Arne. I was more subtle than Arne. And not so smart after all.

The time. Twenty-five minutes. By the front of the hotel sits Vanderslice's limo. What does he have to do with this? I know he's already on the bus, talking to Arne. Laughing with Szabo. Laughing at me. Putting them at ease. Major's nervous, isn't he? Such a nervous man . . .

"Break in the traffic," Beagle says.

I straighten. The bus is a purple bread loaf sitting at the mouth of the drive. Soft rounded corners like the rabbit.

"You sure you're okay, Major?"

"I'm fine."

"You've been up all night. You're probably . . ."

"I'm fine."

I take a step. Ahead, a blue cab pulls around Vander-slice's limo. It pauses behind the bus, unable to clear the drive. The bus's program notices the cab. It inches forward. Wheels swivel right and . . .

world flashes yellow. I'm a man of magic—sailing backward in utter silence. By my out-flung hand a cab powers down and . . .

snapshot of pale balloon face through the windshield. Not bored anymore. Wide eyes. Open mouth. Picture-perfect amazement. My right arm smacks the Permacrete. Something in my side snaps and . . .

look. Oh, look. Swarms of bright comets and bursting black stars.

. . . wait.

Wait a minute.

I don't understand this.

Thought I saw Reece. And now . . . inches away, wheels of a green cab.

What happened? I try to sit up. Balloon face peers at me. A stranger. Open-mouthed. Alarmed.

Beagle. Beagle's here, too. Why am I in the street?

Why does he look so frightened? He leans so close I see the moonscape topography of his cheeks.

His lips move. In my ears an electronic buzz. I can't hear. Damn. Someone turn that down. Pounding agony above my temple. Stabbing pain in my side. Was I knifed?

Sting at my thigh. I put my hand there. Pumping, sticky warmth. I sit up. He tried to kill me, I say, but I can't hear my own voice.

My side hurts. Gummy red on my leg. My palm is painted with it. But farther away. Brighter than that. In front of the hotel a bus is burning.

Did Beagle ask a minute ago if I was tired? I think I am now. Very sleepy. My eyelids droop. So bright. Look, I whisper. Orange flames. Black skeleton of a safety cage. Stench of burning rubber.

More people. All looking. Bots arc streams of water into the flames. White clouds billow. A mound of blue metal melts like warm chocolate.

The buzzing is louder. People staring and I wish they'd stop. Pushy friendliness. Tennysonians. Vanderslice was here a moment ago, wasn't he? Is Mrs. Hendrix all right?

Beagle lays me gently on the pavement. A woman behind him is crying. Lights coming. Red and blue. In strobes.

Beagle looks so worried. That sad-hound face. I close my eyes. The hum in my ears muffles. The pain in my side eases. I remember dreaming about children. A rabbit. Did Reece . . .

Easier than I ever imagined. Easiest, this way. Odd. I always knew I'd be murdered. Funny. I always thought dying would be hard.

18

A loud humming. I open my eyes. White room. Bright lights. Beagle's standing by the bed. His mouth moves.

I gingerly feel around the lump on my head. Touch the Slim Brace around my chest. Put a hand down. On the inside of my thigh, the slick of a surgiclean bandage.

Beagle holds up a Sheet. Across it is written: CAN YOU HEAR ME?

He mouths the words.

No. I shake my head. No.

He erases, writes: THE DOCTOR THINKS THE DEAFNESS IS TEMPORARY.

Better tomorrow. All better, Lila used to say when I'd come home scraped and bruised. And she'd bandage me. Cool kiss on the forehead. Like I was a child. Did she ever want—ever need—children?

My body aches. I close my eyes and drift. Something punches me lightly in the stomach. Beagle leaning over. His lips form: Major?

The burning bus.

Arne? I ask. I can't hear myself. Szabo? I hope I've asked it right.

I must have, because Beagle's cheeks twitch.

We were set up. But who did it? Marvin. Had to be Marvin. Because now Vanderslice, too, is . . .

Marvin was afraid of him, wasn't he? And Vanderslice brought us here without permission. Trying to save himself? Stupid. Stupid. I left the hotel too quickly. Should have waited to hear what Vanderslice was going to say. He was frightened.

Oh, God. For a moment there—what did he know?—he was so frightened.

But I wasn't strong enough for Vanderslice. Not strong enough for the team. My fault. Szabo knew. He was psychic, wasn't he? Knew I was the weak link.

A doctor bustles through the door. Mouth moving at Beagle. Quick mouth. Officious mouth. Brusque orders. A shake of his head and Beagle leaves the room.

The doctor holds something cold to my right ear. Then shoves my cheek into the pillow and holds it to the left. I look out the open door. In the hall Beagle's broad back eclipses someone. Who? They're talking. The shorter, smaller someone takes a nonchalant step to the side.

Half of him now. Hand shoved into the pocket of an expensive Slickstone suit. An extravagant gold band around the wrist. Over Beagle's brown-uniformed shoulder, a glimpse of curly chestnut hair.

I push the doctor's hand away. Push it again. He's startled. I sit up and he tries to stop me. I struggle and he lets me go. When my feet hit the floor my knees try to buckle. A tug at my arm. The doctor. His lips flap angrily. Holding onto the bedpost, the doorjamb, the wall, I wobble out the door.

Now. Peering past Beagle's bulk. Unlined face. Wide green eyes.

Vanderslice!

I know I've screamed because Beagle whirls. Surprised. Nurses at a station turn, mouths agape.

You fucking murderer!

Beagle waves his arm like he's directing my words to a safe place down the hall.

I'll get you for this!

Beagle comes up, puts his hands on my shoulders. Tries to push me into the room. I shove back. But I'm not strong enough. I never was.

I know what you did!

But I'm not sure. They're all lying. They have to be. Beagle too? What if I hadn't seen Reece? Hadn't run . . .

My throat convulses. Did I make a sound? Beagle throws his arms around my shoulders. Stop me. For Christ's sake stop me. I killed them all. Szabo knew that. Everyone, even HF knew.

My throat convulses again. I can't hear the noise I make. But they do. They all hear it. Nurses and doctors are flash-frozen. Vanderslice looks at the carpet.

Then a door down the hall opens. A dead man walks out.

Szabo's blue eyes are wide. His beard, his balding head, are streaked with soot. I see golden afternoon sunlight streaming across the carpet between us. A padded chair lounging against the wall casually as a man waiting on his wife. The red ball in its seat that some child has forgotten.

Beagle lets me go. Stylus in one hand. Sheet in the other.

ARNE. JUST ARNE, he writes.

Just Arne. It's all right. Nothing to worry about. No one, really. Just Arne. I let Beagle steer me to bed.

19

Awake. Beagle's sitting in a chair beside my bed, turning a melted comb over and over in his hands. A red comb. My comb. What interests him in it?

He sees me looking. "Can you hear anything?"

The words come filtered through tinnitus. "A little. Talk louder."

"Can't. Too dangerous. Listen harder." He drops my comb into a box stamped with Gothic letters GW and a sans serif word: EVIDENCE. "You've been sleeping for twenty-four hours straight." He picks something else from the box: a brass parakeet. God's idea of a miracle. Thirty-four people dead in a subway, Arne dead in a bus, and Tinkerbell unscathed.

Beagle regards the bird. Puts it down. "I've stayed in your room. Nobody's had a chance to plant bugs, so we can talk if we keep our voices down. Vanderslice is scared shitless. Tells me over and over that he could have been on board that bus. Would have been, too, if he hadn't followed Szabo into the hotel. The bomb was set to go off automatically when the bus's wheels turned forty-five degrees. What a coincidence."

God's idea of a miracle. Arne. Just Arne.

"You know, Dyle? If the HFCS guy hadn't stayed to see the explosion . . ."

Chemical fire. Hot enough to melt the blue cab. To reduce the bus to a skeleton. That's what he wanted to see. Arsonists like to watch.

"Szabo thought he'd forgotten to pack something. When we went after the HFCS guy, he figured he had time to check his room. He was in the lobby talking to Vanderslice when the bomb went off."

I've strained to catch what he's saying. Now I'm exhausted.

Beagle's words blur. I work to make sense of them. "They ran outside to see. Szabo got hysterical. Tried to get Arne out. Vanderslice dragged him back. Saved his life, probably." Then Beagle says, "Vanderslice wants to talk to you."

The hospital room is tiny, but two Walls make it seem huge. One to my left plays an expansion of the room itself. To my right, behind Beagle, flowers dot a hillside.

I say, "Let's leave."

Beagle doesn't speak.

"We're targets," I tell him. "I don't want to be the reason that a hospital's bombed. Where's Szabo?"

"Here. He shouldn't be alone." His mouth moves again, but the words are too soft.

"I'm deaf, damn it! Don't whisper!"

"Okay. Okay. Don't be so testy. I was just saying that I've never seen such a screwed-up team. We're the walking wounded."

We?

"Szabo's lost it, but he was always close to the brink."

Was he? Maybe I was so close myself that I never noticed.

"They shouldn't have sent him. He can't psychometrize without endwrapping. Didn't HF know that? And Arne. Christ. Nobody could get along with Arne. A demolitions expert with nervous hands and a propensity for paranoia? If the terrorists hadn't killed Arne, he might have ended up killing us himself."

Not Arne. I'm the weak link. I look away. There's something unnatural about that Wall. The lighting. That's it. The light in the Wall doesn't match the light in the room.

A pause, then: "Dyle, it's not just Szabo who can tell how scared you are. Even when there's no reason, I can see your heart rate jump. What the hell is wrong with you?"

The Wall is contrived. Grotesque. There's no life in it.

"Dyle? Listen to me. You have to get your shit together. HF is playing with Vanderslice. They're jerking us around. You're team leader. Act like it. Team leader— God, that chaps my ass. And HF knew it would."

In the artificial Wall a synthetic window looks out on a fraudulent garden.

"We can't let them get by with it. We've been set up, all right. Question is: Why does Earth want us to fail?"

I turn. "Article Five," I say.

"That's right, Dyle. You're thinking now. That's exactly right. It's Article Five. If they let the bombings go on a little longer, Earth will have a reason to put their hands in Tennyson's deep pockets. So when Tennyson asked for help, they sent us. And we looked great on paper.'' Beagle sits forward. His expression is mischievous. ''Know what I think?''

''What?''

''My guess is that the dark secret Vanderslice wants to tell you is that he and Earth have an agreement. I'll bet my M-8 status that Earth is going to let Boy Wonder solve the case and become Chosen of God. But they nearly fucked up. Nearly blew him away. You know what Colonial Security's like. A bunch of goddamned sociopaths. And you know this particular guy well, don't you? Don't you, Dyle?''

My mouth's dry. I run my tongue over my lips. ''No.''

''Tell me the truth.''

''No. Just seen him around. Just know his face.''

''Don't lie to me, goddamn it. I hate that.''

''He scares me, all right? Colonial Security scares me.'' Beagle's voice drops. ''Understood. They scare me, too. Vanderslice probably thought Earth would only act under his orders. But the CS guy is out of control. Either that, or Earth panicked because we're getting close to an answer. Now Vanderslice is scared. He's going to demand that we back off. So do we do what Earth obviously wants us to? Or do we solve this goddamned case?''

I laugh. What else is there to do? ''Okay. Let's solve the fucker.'' And for a moment I really believe we can.

— 20 —

Szabo sits in the cab plucking at his sleeve, not meeting anyone's eyes. His face is drained of color, as if the pale ghost of Arne has burrowed under his skin.

So Szabo loved Arne. They fought, and he walked out, but he still loved him. Now he looks lost—an actor in a film where all the cast but he have memorized their lines. I loved Lila, but we fought, too.

Damn it, Dyle. I don't know you anymore.

So afraid she'd walk out.

You scare me sometimes. The way you look. This case has become an obsession.

What case? Oh. Reece.

The cab stops in front of a sprawling neo-adobe house. Scattered through the neighborhood are spindly pines, no older than the subdivision itself. Foamy-looking maroon groundcover blankets the huge yard. Low hills beyond seem painted a strange bluish-green.

Beagle carries in our bags. I go through the house checking windows. The backyard is unfenced. So open and wide that it's dizzying. In the distance another house. Our closest neighbors—too far away to hear us scream.

I walk down the hall again, steps rapid, and enter a room. Have I been here before? The windows are locked. Blue curtains. Bed with a blue flowered spread. A wall lamp with bunched glass globes. The first time I saw it, it looked cheerful, like grapes. Another time . . . Tears? Is that it? Tears? How many times have I been in here?

I check the nearest window. Forget if I've checked the other, but it's locked, too.

Another room. How many bedrooms are there? The house is too big. The yard's too big. It would take days to find our bodies.

"Dyle?"

Beagle's standing in the doorway, his expression quizzical. "Come eat. You've checked the house now. Everything's all right. Everything's locked."

Is it? Familiar violet curtains. Bedspread gray as ash.

"I made dinner. Come on."

The kitchen. God. Have I checked the kitchen? The room's yellow. It's sunlight and hot chemical fire. I've been in this place before.

Szabo's at the table. His face is grief-stricken. He's not eating. Looks like he's playing my part.

I sit down. Beagle hands me a plate.

"There wasn't anything in my room," Szabo says.

But two windows. All the rooms have at least two windows. I'm hungry. No use. Something's stuck in my throat and I can't get the food down.

"See?" he asks Beagle. "It must have been a psychic warning. I didn't recognize it. If I'd recognized it . . ."

What is he talking about? Why doesn't he shut up? His

voice catches. That barrier. Words can't come up. If you let them, you'll vomit pain.

"You can't keep blaming yourself," Beagle says.

Not Szabo's fault. Mine. If I'd just kept my mouth shut . . . Wait. Did I lock the front door?

There are wet rims at the bottom of Szabo's eyes. "I told Milos to stay in the bus while I went upstairs. Why did I tell him that?"

Beagle says, "It made more sense. It's what I would have done."

"But, damn it. You're not the psychic." Szabo gets up, his expression confused. Forgetting his lines already.

"Where are you going?" Beagle asks.

Befuddled. "I . . . tired. Just . . . lie down for a while."

He walks out.

"Dyle? Aren't you hungry, either?"

"No." I've forgotten something. I go to the patio doors and check to see if they're locked.

"Someone could have thanked me for making dinner."

I see Beagle's reflection in the glass. His voice is as tired as Szabo's.

"You have to eat or you'll get sick. Did you even know what was on your plate?"

Bedspread of ash.

"I've lost Arne. I'll let Szabo slide for now. But you . . . Christ, Dyle. You have to pull yourself together."

He looks frightened. It scares me and I shift my gaze. Outside the patio, the sun is setting. Cirrus clouds in the west wear stripes of red and purple. It looks like the sky is burning.

"I can't do this alone," Beagle says.

"I know."

I check to see if the patio doors are locked. Something—a bird or a bat—flits from the pines and darts, a black silhouette, across the molten Tennyson sun.

"There are patterns here, Dyle. I'm finding patterns. Broken runs of government employees. Of people connected with science. Importers. Exporters. I'm not sure which one's important. If they all are. HF's smart, but not that smart. They can't fool me."

I wasn't so smart, either. Murder. Beagle wrote the book on it.

"Are you listening?"

"I heard every word."

"You have to help," he says.

The sun is a whitish-yellow memory on the underside of the dark clouds.

"Damn it, Dyle! Listen, goddamn it! I can't let them beat me again!"

Again?

In the glass I see Beagle. His face is lowered. Designers gave him a pleasure center; Hoad Taylor, a capacity for pain.

M-8s. I always thought they were safe.

"You need to talk to Vanderslice. But meet him on your terms. He's scared enough so maybe we can turn him."

"No."

"He didn't have anything to do with the bus bombing. I'm sure of it. It was just blind luck that he wasn't killed too."

I shake my head.

Exasperated now. "He's in over his head. He has no idea what HF's like. What they're willing to do . . ."

"He killed Tal Hendrix."

"You don't know that. How the hell could you know that?"

Why else would she talk? "He hurt her."

"You don't know that, either."

"I need to see."

"You mean . . ."

"Go over there and see."

"Look, you're probably still sore. A little rocky from the medication. I don't know whether you should chance going out."

She needs me. Duty is prison. I'll never escape alive.

"It's dark, Dyle. It's getting late."

I can't see the groundcover anymore, the pine trees. Dark out there.

Wait a minute. Have to see if the windows are locked.

"Dyle?"

I stop at the mouth of the hall.

"You look all right, but . . ."

"But what?"

"Not just your injuries—something else. Something's wrong with you."

It sticks in my throat.

"What is it?"

"Nothing."

"Don't shit me, Dyle. I can't see as much as Szabo, but I can tell things. How your pulse rate rises when you talk about Mrs. Hendrix. How your face looked when you saw the HFCS guy. You don't just know him. There's something between you.''

''No.''

''Don't lie to me again. There's no time for that.''

''Colonial Security shouldn't be here. That surprised me. Just surprised me. And Tal Hendrix is important to this case.''

He doesn't believe what I'm saying.

''I just want to interrogate her again.'' See her. Touch her. I have to.

''Well, be careful.'' He sounds doubtful. ''I have to stay here. One of us has to keep an eye on Szabo. And I want to go over those patterns.''

He agrees too easily. I'm trapped. Outside night has fallen. The house is brightly lit. A safe haven. A hot explosion of light.

Before I can lose my courage, I leave. Maybe I'll have the chance to come back. Wonder what I'll find.

21

I take three separate cabs and send them in different directions. By the time I arrive at the Meat Market on God's Gift, it's ten o'clock.

I order the cab to stay. "Tal Hendrix here?" I ask the doorman.

When he answers, "Door three," my knees go watery.

Here. Alive. But the amber light is lit above Mrs. Hendrix's door. I was worried about her, and all the time . . .

So furious that I nearly leave. I stand near the door to Room One and stare at that light. There's a sick cramp up the right side of my body. A throbbing ache behind my eye.

Hold her. All I want to do. Just hold her for a while. Why shouldn't I? I remember how she laughed. Lila had a laugh like that. It forced me to laugh with her. And I'm not a happy man.

Five minutes already. How long will this take? Even if it's a fraud, how can she stand it?

Before Lila, I had cheap whores. Quick blow jobs in dark alleys. Hot mouths. Tight mouths. Felt good. Their faceless heads. I could cup my hands around those skulls and span them. Fragile as eggs. I remember thinking how easy . . .

Are you all right? the last whore asked me.

Fine. I'm fine, I said. *Just a little tired, that's all.*

For a moment I wanted . . .

Did I do something wrong?

I zipped up and paid her. Big tip. Enough money to forget what I'd been thinking. Hated thoughts like that. Sick. Dirty, like the men I arrest. And then Lila, and everything changed. She was so proud, my wife. Always a little aloof. Walks like an M-9, I told Kanz.

Never wanted her like that, never asked that of her. And always wanted to see her face. Look at me, I'd say. I need to remember, I'd think. And I'd keep the lights burning.

The amber above Room Three turns green. The door opens and . . .

God. Vanderslice walks out. What has he done to her? That sick bastard. How could he? Doesn't see me yet. Not smiling. Grim. He's grim. Putting his card back into his wallet.

Have to hide before he sees me. Can't fight. Not hurt like this. I stagger backward. The door to Room One opens and—shit—I'm falling. Reach out. Fumble for the doorjamb. Too late.

I hit the floor with a whoof. Pain knifes through my broken ribs. The door shuts and someone—cheap whore—laughs.

The camera is pointed my way. "Hiding?"

They must see it all the time. "Yes." I clamber awkwardly to my feet.

"Boss? Preacher?"

I think about that. "A boss."

"Want a blow job while you're here? Might as well. You'll have to pay for it, anyway."

"No." Sick fear of what I might want to do.

"Well. Your money."

Vanderslice. Her kneeling before him. Not struggling at all. It might be fair if they fought back. If they had a chance. Fragile skulls in my hand. Not safe to have that power. How could anyone hurt something so . . . Did he? What if she needs me? Maybe he's standing—waiting— just outside the door.

"What kind of uniform is that?"

I've forgotten about her. But she's the kind you can easily forget. I smile gently into the camera. "I'm from Earth."

"Oh. You're kind of cute. And you look so sad. I could cheer you up."

"I'm sure you could."

I check the time. Another five minutes have passed. He's out there. I feel it. When I run my card through the reader, my hand shakes.

"Come back and see me sometime," she says as I leave, and she sounds so lonely.

The hall's empty. The light above Room Three is green. The door opens and I walk through.

"Mrs. Hendrix? It's Major Holloway. Are you all right?"

No answer. I stare at the white wall and see her. Dead in a pool of blood. Funny how something so red, so bright, can look black in the shadows.

"Mrs. Hendrix!"

"Yes?"

"Are you all right?"

Silence. I come closer. Lower my voice. If I could just see her. Touch her. Never hurt her. Never. "Mrs. Hendrix? What did Vanderslice want?"

"What does anyone want here?" Sad voice. Sad room. It smells of quick sex, and dirt cakes the yellowing corners.

"Did he threaten you, Mrs. Hendrix? I have to know."

Faint but unmistakable. The sound of a woman crying. I can't stand to hear it. Can't stand this. "Please. Mrs. Hendrix. Let me help you." How could he do that to her? Have her like that? Faceless. She wouldn't fight. Let him do anything.

"Mrs. Hendrix? I think John Vanderslice may have been responsible for your husband's death. Please. We need to talk. I'm afraid you may be in danger."

A response so quiet I can't understand it.

"I'm sorry? What was that?"

"Go away."

Still crying. Better if I leave now. Afraid to make things worse. I start to tremble. Get him. I'll make him pay for this. I'm shaking so hard I have to run my card through twice before the reader can scan it.

22

The street is empty but for the guard and my cab. The door opens and I crawl inside. Ribs hurt. Head pounds. Endorphin boosters make me sleepy. I watch the dingy streets flash by. The pools of light under the sparse street lamps. I doze and dream about fire and . . .

The cab's stopped. "Cab?"

It doesn't answer.

Shadowy figures at the mouth of an alley. If I could see their faces, I know they'd be . . . Kanz at my shoulder. Face in tight check. So sad. His voice was so sad. *Please, Dyle. Don't look.*

Don't want to dream about this.

A shadow steps off the curb and starts toward me. Click of heels against pavement. Coppery taste of fear in my mouth.

No. No. I'm awake. I'm on the south side of Hebron. Not the alley on M-4. The man's closer. Going to finish the job he started. I'll be murdered here. In the dark.

I palm the door release. It doesn't open. "Cab!"

Big man. Burly. Hand in his jacket pocket. I recognize that stance. Used it before. Can't be. Has a softgun. Not a God's Warrior. Jesus. Colonial Security.

Pound the door with both fists. "Cab!"

A beefy face in the window. The door opens. Gasp of night air. An arm clubs me in the chest. Drives me backward. Sends fireworks of pain through my ribs.

"Minister wants to talk."

Suddenly Vanderslice is here. Climbing inside. Sitting and straightening his jacket. "Hi, Major. How are you feeling? God. You look just terrible."

I bring my fist up fast. Not fast enough. He flinches, and my knuckles barely graze him.

"Hey! Take it easy! What . . ."

Kill him. I'll hurt him like he hurt her. The door behind me opens. I topple backward into space. The man catches me. Arms tight around my chest. Pain like splinters of glass.

"It's okay. I'm fine. Don't hurt him, Kevin."

The grip loosens. I gulp air.

Blood trickles from Vanderslice's nose. He pulls the vanity mirror down from the roof. Daubs at the blood with a handkerchief. "I don't know. Doesn't look broken to me. What do you think, Kev?"

Voice behind my ear. Hot, moist breath. "No, sir. Don't think he broke it."

Vanderslice holds the handkerchief against his upper lip. Studies himself in the mirror. "Why'd you want to do that, Major?"

"Tal Hendrix."

He turns. Wide green eyes. The glow from a nearby streetlight bisects his face. A yin-yang: all goodness and bright above; occult darkness below. "Close the door, Kevin."

"But sir . . ."

"Close the door."

The guard pushes me forward. I nearly fall into Vanderslice's lap. The door slides shut and I lean against it.

"Why Tal?" Vanderslice's nose has stopped bleeding. He folds and then unfolds the handkerchief.

"Son of a bitch. How could you hurt her like that?"

"I never . . ."

"Don't give me that shit. She was crying."

A wince. He looks down at the handkerchief again.

"You threatened her. You . . ."

"No. Come on."

"Abandoned her there. Jesus Christ. How could you do that? That job . . . what she does. She was married to a scientist. Must have had a good life up until now. How can you let her degrade herself like—"

"Degrade?" A surprised laugh. "No, Major. No, no. She likes it."

A rush of fury and adrenaline. He sees my fists bunch and throws up his hands.

"Hold it. Just cool off, okay? The Meat Markets are—"

"I know."

"Don't be so angry. It's all done by machine—"

"That makes it all right? They're still using her. She's still—" A faceless, nameless fuck. "She's nothing to them. Just a—" Hot mouth.

Nodding. Trying to get a word in. "Right. Right. I agree with you. But Tal thinks it's funny."

"Funny?" The word deafens me.

"Well, I suppose there's something pretty absurd about the whole thing, really. If you stop and think about it. She keeps the camera on them so she can see their faces. And there's the man on one side of the wall, with his . . . Okay. You've been there. You get the picture. And that machine on the other, chugging away. Tal says she has to bite her lip to keep from laughing. So. There you have it. Funny. A big joke. And when it's all over, she tells them how good they were. How big. You know the kind of stuff . . ."

Whore talk.

"Go figure. But she tells me it gives her a sense of power."

No one should have power like that.

"Hey, look. It wasn't my idea. I didn't want her to work there. But women don't have any rights. And she refused to let a man—any man—take care of her."

I was worried about her. Felt sorry for her. And all the time she wanted to. Liked it. Thought everything was a joke.

"She couldn't sign the papers to get the insurance money. Couldn't transfer the house deed into her name. 'Fuck them,' she told me. And she does. Every night. And bites her lip to keep from laughing."

Vanderslice reaches into his pocket. A softgun? Does he have a softgun? Or clandestine orders from Colonel Yi?

Stupid. I'm so utterly fucked I have to bite my lip to keep from laughing. This goes higher than Yi. It goes right to the Executive Council. To the Prime Minister. That's how far it has to go.

Vanderslice brings out a tin. Opens it and offers it to me. "Z-Tabs," he says. "Want one?"

What's he trying to pull? "They're illegal."

"God, Major. Really." He sets a Z-Tab on his tongue and puts the tin away. "I've been taking them for my nerves."

A motion in the shadows. I tense. One of Vanderslice's plainclothes God's Warriors patrolling the street.

I say, "All right. Get to the point. Just give me my orders."

A sigh from the dark. "No sense ordering you back to the hotel, I suppose. Security's been breached." Vanderslice's words slur. His eyes are half-staff. Already in the grip of the drug.

My eyes follow the guard as he walks behind the cab.

"Listen. I don't know what Tal said to you, but Paulie was my friend."

What's the guard doing back there? "The editorials—"

"No, no, no. Not the editorials. Haven't you figured it out? I told him to write those."

Wait. Wait a minute.

"Paulie was working for me."

Everything falls apart. Everything. My world shatters.

"Paulie kept an eye on things for me. He wrote the editorials as cover. You've heard of our unrest here. People are disgruntled. Happens in a theocracy. Paulie was apolitical. Loved science. Didn't love Tal like that. A shame, but that was okay. She never loved him, either."

Didn't love him. Never any grief on her face. Not like in Szabo's. In mine. They lived together. Never loved each other. And then he died. So pathetic.

"She married him so she wouldn't have to have children. It's expected of women here. But he never wanted children, never wanted a wife. They were partners, sort of. Liked each other a lot. Anyway, Paulie gave me names. No one knew, not even the God's Warriors."

The guard moves to the sidewalk. Peers into the alley. "Did she know?"

"Tal?" He shrugs. "Couldn't tell her the whole story. She would have put two and two together."

"What do you mean?"

"Oh, disappearances. That kind of thing."

No capital punishment on Tennyson. That's what the files say. No capital punishment. But . . . "You kill people. Paulie Hendrix gave you the names of the revolutionaries, and you killed them."

He rolls his eyes. "It's my job. Protecting Marvin. And so what? Big deal. Come on, Major. Stop looking at me like that. You can't let anarchists run loose. Four. Okay? Four anarchists. And a few more murderers or so. Marvin really believes that crap about Christian charity. He thinks God turns your life around. You know better. Poor Marv lives in a dream world."

Paulie Hendrix gave him names. Vanderslice killed them. Tal never loved. Not really. Laughed more than she grieved.

"That's why I know the evidence the God's Warriors found is bogus. I know the revolutionaries. They hold their little secret meetings. They sit around and complain about Marvin. But now somebody's getting into DEEPs. Somebody's making and setting off bombs without leaving DNA markers. How does somebody do that? Even the smartest criminal screws up every once in a while. And where are the explosives coming from? Listen, Major. I know everything and everybody who sets foot on this planet. I know to the gram where our home-grown chemicals are. See what I mean? How does that happen?''

He daubs at his nose. Does it hurt? Can anything, anything at all, hurt him?

''Why did you leave the hotel like that?'' Annoyed at me now. Not angry. Not murderous. Just annoyed. ''I had everything set up. All my men were in place. All the surveillance. And then you go and mess things up. And I nearly got on that bus. Do you realize that? Made my men jumpy. So I'd watch it, Major. Just a friendly warning. And another piece of advice: I expect you to keep me up to date on what you find. Understand?''

My breath stops as the plainclothes guard approaches. He raps lightly on the window and points at his watch.

''Oops. Have to go. Marv's expecting some sort of report. He's frantic. Thinks God's testing him. Go figure. So, we're communicating now, right? No games?''

Talia Hendrix wasn't laughing. She was crying. I heard her cry.

The guard taps the cab's hood. Vanderslice nods at him. Holds up a finger. ''There'll be a contingent of my guards around you at all times. They'll try not to be conspicuous. They'll stay out of your way. But I'm not letting you out of my sight.''

He gets out and walks across the street. The door slides

shut. A guard steps from the shadows, lifts something. Points it. The cab leaps forward.

I look back. Vanderslice and his men have already melted into the darkness. Two blocks down a cab is trailing me.

23

The cab drops me in front of the neo-adobe. I look back, but can't see the other cab. Better than I expected, the undercover God's Warriors. More dangerous. And Vanderslice is more deadly than I'd ever believed.

The door opens. I limp into the darkened living room. Beagle's standing by a lamp in the den. "You look like shit. Sit down, Dyle. I'll get your pills."

I collapse into an overstuffed chair. Beagle brings me iced water and a white tablet. He sits and watches me take it.

"I got the pattern," he says. "And I was wrong. It's all centered around Paulie Hendrix."

I bobble the glass. My hand's shaking too much to hold it. I set it on an end table.

"Solving this one was a real hard-on, Dyle. There were patterns within patterns like a Chinese puzzle box."

A whir. Something lumbers at me—right at me—from the shadows. Beagle turns in surprise. The household bot. Just the bot. It rolls over, sets a doily under my glass, then moves to a parking place against the wall.

Beagle's shoulders relax. "So. The pattern. Drs. Kenneth J. Battle and Valentin Popek, partners in quantum physics, were killed in blast number one. They had recently sold an article to *Godly Science*. Morgan Berstermann, part-time typist and full-time homemaker, was killed in blast two. She did a bit of freelance copy editing on the sly. Women aren't supposed to have jobs here. But she was safe, I suppose, with Hendrix. Blast three got rid of Shulton Gaddis. Gaddis's job was transferring data from computers to insertable Sheet tabs. And we can guess who one of his clients was.''

"Four was Paulie himself.''

"Yes. And five was one I'm particularly proud of. Lennie Brooksfielder was hard to track, but I finally nabbed him. Anything used was Lennie's game. A bit of shuckster, a bit of shade-tree mechanic was Lennie. *Godly Science* worked on a shoestring budget, and when the magazine needed a new liquid crystal color plater, guess who they went to? Fortunately all IST equipment needs to be registered with the government or I never would have found him. Anyway, eight months before his death, Lennie sold Hendrix the equipment. Three weeks before his death the luckless Lennie was called in to fix it. The warranty was still good.''

"And six?''

"Six was tough. A computer artist by the name of Greel Iovinelli. He'd never done work for the magazine, but I found an electronic check. It wasn't a chit from *Godly Science*, either, but a personal bank transfer from Hendrix. The *Godly Science* account was overdrawn by the time Iovinelli needed paying, and Hendrix paid him out of his home budget.'' Beagle chuckles. "Great shit, huh? And seven was Dr. Thurgood Ezekiel Daws, physicist and part of the peer jury *Godly Science* used to determine the printability of its articles. Eight was Golden Thompson, no Ph.D., but so widely accepted as an expert in his field that he was part of the peer jury, too.''

Eight. The bomb blast we investigated. Was Thompson the hand in the rubble? The puddle of blood under the wall?

Beagle says, ''And we were nine.''

I wipe my hands down my face. ''What does it mean?''

''Don't know yet. The missing article bothers me, but I still say our favorite boy spy is out to kill the Chosen and HF's helping him. Remember, Vanderslice is also a scientist. He probably directed the bombings. He published in *Godly Science*, at least before he changed careers. So . . . jealousy?''

''There's an article missing?''

''The article by Battle and Popek that *Godly Science* bought is nowhere to be found. I checked their DEEPs— the obvious place to hide something—but they were empty. I figure Vanderslice got into there and erased Battle and Popek's work.''

''Why?''

''Goddamn it, Dyle!'' His face twists in anger, and I realize I've pricked his vanity. ''I told you I don't know! From what I hear, Battle and Popek were brilliant. I know Daws and Thompson were. Vanderslice knew them well. Shit, he attended off-planet conferences where they were speakers.''

''Vanderslice cornered me tonight.''

Beagle's startled. ''What did he want?''

"Just to talk. It was all talk. Fed me a bunch of shit. Told me . . ." That she likes it. That she watches and laughs.

"Told you what, damn it?"

"That Paulie was working for him the whole time." That she never loved him. Never. "Said he gave him names of people who were dissatisfied with the government. Vanderslice got rid of some of them."

"He had you alone, then? No witnesses?"

"Just his own guards."

"Why didn't he kill you?"

Kill me? I'm stunned. I shouldn't be.

"This has me worried." Beagle shakes his head. "With what I've found out, I'm not sure we can turn him. Still, it looks like Boy Wonder and HFCS had a little falling out. He knows the plant here is out of control. Wants us to find him. Maybe he wants out of the contract. By the way. I have a line-up for you to look at. The HFCS guy was tall. He had reddish hair. That's all I could see before he ran off. I gathered all the males fitting that description who were approached by the infamous holo bimbo this year. There are fifty-two. Want to take a look, or are you ready for bed?"

"I'll look."

Beagle goes to his workstation and hits the power button. "It's all set up. I'll get you a cup of coffee."

I change chairs slowly. My body's sore.

By the time Beagle comes back I'm at number thirty-three and my eyes are tired. Beagle pulls up a chair, sets a cup near me. "You're almost through. Nothing yet?"

"No." I tap the space bar. Picture of a middle-aged

man with a receding hairline, wild disgust on his face. "Remember Reece Wallace?"

"Of course. You made him famous, didn't you? Everyone remembers Reece."

"That's who he looks like." I scroll up a laughing teenager. Beagle doesn't speak. "I don't know what he looked like before the doctors changed him. But now he has Reece Wallace's face."

I scroll up another man. Another. Then another. Won't he say something?

"Your pulse rate shoots up every time you hear his name. I know it was a bitch of a case, but what . . . Hold it. You think Reece Wallace killed your wife, don't you?"

Cold. So cold my spine goes taut. "No."

"But you link them somehow. I can tell. Is that because they never solved her homicide? You play her murder over and over in your mind. You relive it. And you have to give the villain a face."

I pound the space bar hard. END OF ENTRIES flashes across the screen.

"Isn't that right?"

"The HFCS guy. They planted an EPAT on him. That's why the holo never took his picture."

"Dyle? Is it?"

I shut my eyes.

"Does HF know about this? They have to, don't they? It would come up in your annual psychological test. And that's why they MedAltered this guy."

Deaf to it. Blind.

"You tried to solve her homicide yourself, didn't you. Tried to find the murderer, but—"

''No damned clues! Goddamn it! What do you expect from me? There weren't any clues!''

''I know. I know that.''

''What do you know? Fuck you. You don't have any idea. My own friends tried to make . . . told me to forget about it. Forget? Oh, Jesus Christ! Forget? They could handle it. Take care of everything. Oh, sure. Sure.'' The room blurs. I'm blind.

''Dyle . . .''

''Shut up. How can you know? You don't know.'' Loved her. For a year and a half I've grieved more than laughed. So pathetic.

''Listen to me. He was dead long before Lila was murdered. You looked for Reece six years. One hundred and seventy-five murders. A hundred and seventy-five autopsies. Bloody murder scenes. Six years. Finding Reece must have obsessed you. Difficult cases do that. Dyle? Don't you see what HF's doing?''

Shut the hell up! Did I get the words out? I blunder to my feet. Can't see the room. Just streaks of light and dark.

''HF knows Reece scares you.''

Knock over a chair. A table. Where's the door? The goddamned door? Hand on my arm. Grip so tight it hurts. ''Dyle? Reece couldn't have killed Lila.''

My groping fingers touch a wall. Cool. Smooth. Simple to understand. I lean my hot cheek against it. ''I know.''

24

In a magstation. Where was I headed? The destination board is a blur. And I've lost my ticket. Can't have. Damn it. Stranded if I can't find that ticket. Can't go anywhere if . . .

Touch on my shoulder. Someone behind me. Lila. No one else would dare . . . Oh. That's stupid. I was so worried about being stranded, but I was holding the oranges, after all.

She tries to put her hands over my eyes. I push them away. The bag drops from my arms and oranges roll every direction. See what she made me do? Now I'll never get them back in the bag. Have to find . . . But why? Not all the oranges are important.

Playing that game again. I slap her hands from my eyes and turn. Not Lila. John Vanderslice behind me.

Blood gushes from his nose. Spills over the front of his suit. His hands are red with it. "You're so funny," he says and he laughs. "You're just so funny, Major."

Blood covers the floor. It's slippery. Hard to keep my balance, but still, I laugh with him. Laugh until I'm weak.

• • •

I wake with a vague feeling of contentment, and look at the time twice before I believe. I slept until four in the afternoon.

Yawning, I walk to the bathroom. I stretch. Take off my pajamas. The Slimcast is beginning to turn color. Tomorrow I'll be able to remove it. Odd how good I feel. By the time I shower and shave, I'm hungry. No. I'm starved.

Szabo's door is closed. Beagle's at his workstation. I put on coffee and look through the pantry. Pizza. Fat baroque cherubs on the package. Nearly full-frontal cherub nudity, if not for the red letters over each crotch. Mushroom. Green pepper. And—unintentionally funny?—Italian sausage.

I read the instructions. Put it in the oven. Jesus. Sausage.

"Cosmology."

Beagle's standing in the kitchen doorway.

"Cosmology?"

"Well, well. Aren't we in a good mood today? Golden Thompson was an expert in cosmology. Why would he be peer-reviewing Battle and Popek's work? They were quantum physicists. The immense passes judgment on the incomprehensibly tiny?"

The oven blats. I reach inside. The package is cool. The pizza inside burns my fingers. Thick crisp crust. Lots of cheese.

"Maybe the article's not important, but I loathe missing puzzle pieces," Beagle says. Before I can separate the slices, he's plucked a mushroom and popped it in his mouth. "What do you think?"

"I'm wondering if you can taste that."

A nod. "You bet. Great shit. Put some of that parmesan and red pepper on it. Don't look at me like that. I don't digest it, for Christ's sake. And water'll flush it out. Anyway, Popek was separated from his wife. Battle, the child genius, dated like a buck rabbit but never the same woman twice. I've talked to Golden Thompson's wife on the phone. Nice lady, but I sense she adds and subtracts the house budget on her fingers. Her only impression of her late husband's prize-winning work was that he seemed somewhat interested in stars. She did, however, remember seeing a delivery with Battle's return address on it. A manuscript-sized delivery. You do see the importance of that."

"Odd." I pry away a triangle and lift it, trailing strings of mozzarella to my mouth. Steam rises. Oregano and garlic. That little restaurant we used to . . . What was the name? Lila always got the lasagna. Always the lasagna. I ordered something different each time, and she'd steal forkfuls of mine.

The pizza isn't as good as I hoped. Not as good as in that restaurant.

"Intriguing, right?" Beagle asks.

"Have the rest of that." I rummage through the cabinet again. Tuna. Albacore tuna? Is it the same fish? Artichoke hearts? What do they mean, artichoke hearts?

"Sure you don't want it?"

"Not as good as restaurant pizza."

"Bullshit. This is restaurant pizza. What sort of restaurants do they have on M-4, anyway? This is real Italian sausage. Loaded with anise."

"Fennel. Italians put fennel in their sausage."

"I'm talking about the stuff that tastes like licorice."

"Right. Fennel."

He makes a disgruntled, maybe a dubious sound. "You get a load of the painting on the box?"

"Baroque. Probably Titian."

"Giotto. You don't have taste buds for shit, Dyle," he says through a full mouth. "I think the trank packs they prescribed for Szabo are too strong."

"Why?" Fried shrimp. Wonder what it tastes like? Breading so light it looks like gold clouds. And cocktail sauce. The red stuff. Interesting, but . . .

"He's sleeping too much. Never gets out of bed. Christ. Since the bombing, he hasn't even taken a goddamned shower."

"Oh . . ." Maybe a steak? "That's what you do."

"What the hell kind of response is that? What the hell do you mean 'that's what you do'?"

"You know. Trying to get through things. When Lila . . ." My hand freezes on a Chinese dinner. General Tso's chicken with shrimp spring roll. I've never talked about this. Not with anyone. And then somehow, it's so easy. "When Lila died," I say and my voice doesn't waver, "they gave me the standard two weeks off. Stayed in bed. Don't think I even brushed my teeth. It's what you do."

I hear him chewing.

"Come on, Beagle. It's what you do."

"Okay. But he's not eating, either."

"You don't eat." I put a package of lobster down.

Sauce looks too rich. Strawberry jam. Maybe just toast and strawberry jam.

"Send him home, Dyle."

Jar in hand, I turn. "Why?"

The pizza is gone. Crumbs cover the plate. Clot of tomato sauce. Mushroom in a pale shroud of cheese. "He's an impediment."

"For Christ's sake. Give him time."

"We don't have time. Besides, I'm worried about him."

"So you'd send him back? What would he go home to? M-0 Level housing. An M-0 Level of a life."

"I think he's going crazy. I think he's going to commit suicide. And then what? What do we do about that?"

"Oh." No. Not toast. Back to my rummaging again. Something in here should look good. Something . . . "You know how it is."

Silence.

"Everybody thinks about killing themselves sometimes. You know what it's like."

I look around. He doesn't know. Never once contemplated it.

"I'm afraid to leave him alone."

"Why? Thinking about something is different than doing it. You just think about it, okay, Beagle? That's all you do. After Lila died," I say and the words slip through my lips as though they had no meaning, no history, no warmth, "walking across the room was a major event. Getting up in the morning was a big fucking deal. Everything was hard. Steps were higher. Silverware was heavier. You don't kill yourself because it would take too much energy. You don't kill yourself because you'd have to make a decision. All you can do is . . ." Tears in my eyes. Shit. Didn't realize I was about to cry. I turn away quickly before he sees.

Tiredly. "Yeah, I know. You go over and over what happened."

What a shame. He doesn't know. Never loved. A shame. "No, Beagle. You don't. You spend every bit of energy not thinking about it."

A sound in the hall. Szabo shuffles into the kitchen, a terry-cloth robe flapping around him.

"How you feeling?" Beagle asks with such forced heartiness that I wince.

Szabo's gaze wanders from the wall to the table. To the counter. To the empty plate.

"Szabo? Hey? Szabo? Want something to eat?"

Dull eyes. To the refrigerator. To the floor. To the salt shaker.

"Well, okay. That's fine. Go ahead and sit down. I'll fix something. A steak? Want a steak?"

Beagle walks around him. Szabo stands there, deaf and blind. I remember how huge grief used to be. How confusing. A littered monochrome world, like the subway after the blast.

"Hey, look! A New York strip steak. You like steaks. I remember that. Comes with a spinach salad and garlic bread and a baked potato." Beagle puts the package in the oven. "This rental's a wet dream. You should see how the cabinets are stocked. Lobster. Caviar. For Christ's sake. Can you imagine? Caviar. Had it once. Hated it."

Szabo pulls his bathrobe tighter. It's too hard to look

at him. I move my attention to the counter. To the brewed coffee. To the strawberry jam. I'm not hungry any-more.The oven blats. It startles me. When I look around, Szabo's gone.

"I've been thinking," I tell Beagle. A lie. Haven't thought about it until this second. "The drunk I told you about in the bar—"

"Yeah. Why'd he walk away like that? Crap. Who's going to eat all this?" He takes the package from the oven. Opens it.

I pick up the garlic bread. Suddenly I have the urge to do something. Go somewhere. It's impossible to stand still. "Listen to me. Listen, Beagle. The drunk in the bar. Know what he said?"

"No, Dyle. I don't fucking know what he said."

Go somewhere. Do something. I take a bite of bread. Butter runs down my fingers. Parsley. Parmesan. Crisp on the outside, soft within. Mixture of opposites like . . .

Exasperated. "You have my complete and utter atten-tion. What the hell did he say?"

. . . like Lila used to be. "He said Earth was a bright place."

"He was a goddamned drunk, Dyle. Probably every-thing looked bright."

I put the bread down. "But he got the patch from somewhere, didn't he. And we know he didn't go to Earth." If he'd seen Earth, he'd know. He'd know. Not even a drunk could make it radiant. "We have to talk to him. Don't you see—"

"Oh, Christ in a handbasket." Beagle's eyes widen and I'm glad for him. He's back to familiar territory, back to something he can understand. "Colonial Security has to have a command center here."

25

We sit in the cab, shoulders touching.

"I hate to leave Szabo like this," Beagle says.

Brilliant, but he doesn't understand. An itchy, anxious energy up my spine. Anticipation in my gut. Dim south side streets flash by. What's Beagle saying now? Oh. Still talking about Szabo.

"He'll be all right." My mind is supernaturally sharp. It jumps from problem to problem, and I understand everything. "He's out of the loop now. A cipher. Vanderslice doesn't need to get rid of him, and he's too depressed to hurt himself."

Something under the street lamp. A small dog running loose. Why did his owners let him out? Something so valuable like that. Then I see patches of hair missing. Raw skin beneath. He's sick. The little dog's sick. If Lila and I had a dog like that, we'd take care of him better. Brush him until his coat gleamed.

The dog looks at the cab. Its eyes are big and sad and brown.

"What the hell's the matter with you, Dyle?"

Did he see me crying?

"Quit drumming your fingernails on the door like that," Beagle says. "You're driving me crazy."

Only then do I notice what I'm doing. I put my hands in my lap. It seems like we've been riding for hours.

"Now you're fucking jiggling your foot. Will you stop? Just settle down."

At Divine Mercy the cab halts. I'm out and walking across the street. Beagle shouts at me to wait. I left him to pay. I forgot to pay the cab.

Then he's out of the cab and striding toward me. I open the door to the restaurant. Four men in overcoats hunch at the end of the counter. When we walk in, they leave their food, their drinks. They sidle quickly past. Chalky face on one. Rouge and red lips on another. Sidelong appraising glances, and they're gone.

"You again," the barkeep says. A hamburger patty sizzles on the grill. There's a spatula in her hand. The air smells of onions and years-old grease.

I slap my card on the counter. "Cheeseburger. Whiskey."

She scans the card. Puts a bottle and chipped glass next to my hand. The liquor's colorless. It burns down my throat, and leaves no aftertaste.

"We need the name and the address of the man I was talking to when I was in here last."

She has beady eyes and nervous hands. She looks at Beagle. At me. Then puts another patty on the grill. "Write your name and number in the bathroom. That's what men do when they want a backed heave-ho."

I pour myself another glass. Drink it down. She puts a slice of cheese atop the meat and I watch the corners melt.

I want the hamburger so bad I can't stand it.

"Tell me his name," I say.

"Sure you want to two-time your boyfriend that-a-way?"

She grills the bread. Puts the sandwich together. Sets it in front of me. I take a bite and swallow. The food nearly comes up again.

"The name."

She leans her belly against the counter. Arms folded under her breasts. "You don't scare me, you know. You can't push me around like—"

Snatch her wrist. Bring her arm down hard. Elbow cracks against counter. Pain and surprise wash her face. I twist her wrist until she cries out. Until muscles and tendons bulge.

"Dyle!"

Feels too good to stop. Hand on the back of her head. Shove her face down. Jaw hits with a wet smack. Jerk her up by the hair. Blood splatters the counter.

"Je-sus!"

Strong arms pull me away. The woman's bleeding from the mouth. Bit her tongue. They usually do. The bottle has fallen over, and a puddle of clear liquor spreads on the bar, turns the blood pink.

"Dayton Pearcy," she says, wiping her mouth.

"Ma'am? Are you all right?" Beagle asks.

"Name's Dayton Pearcy."

"Where?" I ask.

"Lives above the Alleluia Hair Salon on He Shall Reign. Two blocks north. One block east. Room eight. Third floor."

Beagle pulls me outside. "Jesus Christ, Dyle. What do you think you're doing?"

I jerk my arm away and start walking north.

"What's the matter with you?"

He trots to keep up. I could run to where Dayton Pearcy lives. I could run all night, all day. Nothing can stop me.

"I read your files," Beagle's saying. "Tough investigator. But I thought you were goddamned smarter than this. You can't pull shit like that. You embarrassed me. It's such bad manners. Dyle? This isn't Earth. Are you listening?"

The Alleluia Hair Salon is darkened and security-meshed for the night. Next to the door is a rickety two-person lift. Beagle and I squeeze inside.

"Let me handle Pearcy," Beagle says.

The lift opens. The third floor corridor is seedy. Paint peels from the Permacrete. The hall stinks of urine and cheap food.

The door to eight is missing. A stained blanket hangs in its place. Beagle knocks on the wall, just under the chipped number. At the far end of the corridor, behind the door to eleven, a small dog starts to yap.

He calls, "Mr. Pearcy?"

With a shriek the door to nine opens. An elderly woman looks out.

"Mr. Pearcy?"

No answer. I flip aside the blanket. We walk in.

The apartment is a one-room affair. On a mattress near a smudged window, Dayton Pearcy is snoring.

Beagle kneels and prods his shoulder.

The man's eyes fly open. He moves so fast Beagle's

grasping hand misses. But I'm quick. And everything's so easy. I catch him, slam him against the wall.

"You remember me?"

"No."

"I bought you a drink. You remember me?"

"No." Pearcy struggles. I hold him by the throat. Just under the Adam's apple. One squeeze and . . . God, I want . . .

Beagle pulls me away.

Pearcy crawls to his mattress and curls up in the corner. "Don't hurt me."

"No, sir," Beagle says. "You'll be all right. We're not going to hurt you."

"You guys are always after me."

Beagle kneels near him. "Us?"

"A guy like you."

"Tell me what he looks like."

"Badass. Mean look to him."

"What color's his hair?"

"Reddish. The kind of red gals color to. Nice color red."

"His eyes?"

The drunk laughs. Looks at me. His smile dies. "Shit. Don't you guys know?"

Beagle says, "Just tell us the color of his eyes."

"Not dumb enough to get that close."

"Heavy set?"

Pearcy gives it some thought. "Don't know."

Beagle brings an ID kit out of his pocket. "Flip through. See if you see him."

Pearcy thumbs the scroll button.

"This one," he says and hands the kit to Beagle.

On the lighted screen, the official HF front and side post-arrest views of Reece Wallace.

Beagle asks, "Why's he after you?"

"You nuts? He wants to kill me."

"Why?"

"'Cause he knows I been to Earth. Jesus."

"When? When were you on Earth?"

"Couple a weeks ago."

"Where?"

"Down in the subway tunnels, that's where Earth is." Pearcy rummages around in the soiled sheets and comes up with the HF patch. "Nobody believes me, but I snatched it off him. That proves it. Bastard don't wear his uniform around here no more, you bet."

Beagle takes the patch, but Pearcy snatches it away. "Nobody believes me, but I know. I seen. Earth's a big room with people in it with uniforms on like you."

"Just like ours?"

"Puke green. I like this brown color better."

Beagle says, "Where is this Earth you saw?"

"Subway tunnels, dincha hear good? Shit. You're from there. What's the matter? Can't find your asshole with a map and a Glo-Lite?"

"Where in the subway tunnels?"

"Donno. Could be anywheres. Don't remember."

I bend down. Look into his eyes. He leans away. "Where?"

Beagle puts an arm between me and Pearcy. "Listen, Mr. Pearcy. People are dying on Tennyson. You've heard about the bombings?"

"Yeah. Yeah." Fast, emphatic nods.

"Well, all right. We want the bombings to stop, you understand? If Earthers are doing it, then we want to know. And you can help us."

Pearcy looks at me again.

"My friend here just hates bombings. You can understand that, can't you?"

Pearcy's head dips.

"I won't let him hurt you, if you just tell me where Earth is."

Pearcy's bloodshot eyes meet Beagle's. "I forget."

I shove Beagle out of the way. Grab the collar of Pearcy's sweater.

"I forget, okay? I forget stuff lately. Earth could be anywheres. I go scavenging, see? Picking up tools somebody's forgot and stuff. There's a whole maze of tunnels. Could be anywheres between Romans 1 and Ecclesiastes 6."

Beagle pushes me off him. "He's talking about the maintenance tunnels."

Out the streaked windows, a hysterical whoop-whoop. Pearcy wrenches his head around. "What's that?"

Beagle says, "Just sirens. How far do you go on your hunting expeditions?"

Pearcy looks confused. "Sirens?"

My mind's so fast. More nimble than Beagle's. I take out my cuffs. Fasten one end to the thick strap on the side of the mattress.

Beagle says, "Dyle? What are you doing?"

Nimble thoughts. They bounce from one problem to another. Sirens on the south side. But Pearcy will never get this mattress through that door. I seize his wrist and cuff it. "Let's see what's happened, Beagle. Right now. He's not going anywhere."

We leave. As we get into the lift, I hear the dog in apartment eleven. His barks are frenzied.

26

On the street I stop, confused. Echoes distort the sirens. Beagle cocks his head. Listens. "This way." And he hurries toward Deliverance.

Two long blocks and then, ahead, red strobes wash the buildings. It looks like the street's aflame. We round the corner. Three service trucks are parked outside the Meat Market on God's Gift. My steps falter.

Beagle turns. "Dyle?"

Panic squeezes the air from my lungs. God's Warriors, green uniforms lurid in the strobes. A group of them, holding Riot Busters, even though the streets are empty.

I take a shambling step. Then another. So tired all of a sudden.

A God's Warrior sees us coming. "Move on. Move—" As we enter the light, his frown changes to open-mouthed surprise.

"What's happening, officer?" Beagle asks.

He shrugs. "A homicide."

I push past. Just inside, the beefy doorman is surrounded by skeptical cops. Room Three is open, the light burning green for AVAILABLE. Too bright. So bright here. Not an alley, but . . . a cluster of officers. One with a holocam. A man with CORONER across his jacket.

A murmured question from a cop behind. The door-guard's quiet: "Tall. Reddish hair. Early forties."

A God's Warrior with gold braid is leaving Room Three. His eyes lock with mine. Not Kanz. Not Gonzales. Not Anders. They were so sad. And he's not. Then I recognize the nose. Danny. From bombing number eight.

"On time for this one, aren't you, Tick? Only this is an internal matter." He blocks my path. Face to face. Does he really think I want in there? I know better now. If you look, you remember the blood. You remember everything.

Beagle plants a hand on his chest and shoves him back. "Who's dead?"

"Don't push me, Tick. Don't do that."

"Who?"

"Whore. Murdered by someone from Internal Safety, so it doesn't concern you. Or would you care to go in and impede the investigation?"

"Internal Safety?" Beagle asks.

"Secret police."

"You have the perp in custody?"

The cop runs a hand through his cropped hair. "Not yet."

"How do you know it was Internal Safety?"

"Choice of weapon."

I understand so easily. I push him aside.

"Hey! What are you—"

The police photographer turns. Man from the Coroner's office swivels. Faces . . .

Not sad.

"Hey!"

A God's Warrior leans against the wall of Room Three. I'm nimble. Doesn't have time to stop me.

They're taking the wall down. Behind. On the floor. A woman's body, arms tucked to her chin. Rigid, contorted face. No blood. Doesn't look like Tal Hendrix anymore. Death does that sometimes. Didn't look like Lila, either, for a second.

A discolored patch in the white where the energy hit. Doesn't look like her. Can death have changed her that much? Black hair. Blue eyes. Thin body.

"Dyle?" Beagle calls.

I dart past Beagle. Run down the corridor to the doorman. I grab his apron and nearly pull him off his feet. "Where's Tal Hendrix?"

"Sick day. She took a sick day."

Someone puts a hand on my shoulder. Jerks me around. Danny. "What do you know about this?"

I knock him backward. Walk to the front door. Have to get to her. Warn her before it's too late.

"Stop that man!"

Three God's Warriors fall on my shoulders. Drag me to my knees. The front door opens and a well-dressed north sider walks in. "Earthers? You brought in the Home Force? God's love! What did you do that for?"

Arms pulled behind my back. Trying to cuff me. I slam my shoulder into a cop's chest and drive him into a wall.

The north sider bends down to me, nervously explaining. "I take every precaution. I'm registered. We have security cameras for this sort of thing."

Danny grabs the man's jacket. Flings him aside. "Major? You either tell me what you know or you're under arrest. Make up your mind."

"Will someone please call John Vanderslice?" Beagle asks.

Danny's head snaps to Beagle.

"Is there a phone in here, sir?"

The north sider points up the hall. Danny knocks the man's arm down hard. "There's no need to bother the Minister."

Beagle lifts an eyebrow. "Oh. How silly of me. I thought since you were accusing one of his own men of murder he might be interested."

The businessman is rubbing his arm. He looks from Beagle to Danny to me. "It's all good clean fun. Really. If the man discovered that no sex was being exchanged, he could have asked for his money back. Killing one of the girls seems like sour grapes."

A cop to my right blushes. His face falls in disillusioned shock. His expression is so funny.

Danny says, "Okay. Let him go."

The cops take their hands off me. I'm laughing so hard Beagle has to help me to my feet.

"That's two, Major," Danny says. "At three, I'll take you behind a building somewhere. We'll see if you think a few zaps with a Buster is funny."

Laughing. Can't walk. Can't catch my breath. I stagger, bump Beagle's side. Try to speak, but wheeze instead. My stomach hurts. Not Tal. Never was Tal. Shot through the wall and never knew. What an asshole.

"Dyle. Will you just stop?" Beagle grabs my arm and

steadies me as I stumble. Cool air of the street. Dim lights. Round, curious faces.

I try to stop laughing. I try. But my belly quivers. The next thing I know, I'm howling again. Tal was right. It's so damned funny. That cop. That blush. Never saw behind the wall. Never, ever knew.

27

I hurry toward Divine Mercy. "We're getting Mrs. Hendrix right now. We're bringing her back to the house."

"I don't know if that's a good idea. Dyle? You hear me?"

Won't listen.

He screams, "Stop thinking with your dick, goddamn it!"

I whirl. Slam my fist into his stomach. Soft mock flesh; underlying metal. He falls back against a wall. Hurts me more than it does him. My knuckles throb. But he's surprised. Not as tough as I thought. Not nearly as smart. "I'm team leader. I give the orders."

"Orders? You think there's any order left? Any rules? We're in this on our own. Don't you see that? We can't trust anyone. We don't know crap about this woman."

"Vanderslice wants to kill her."

"If he wanted to kill her, she'd be dead by now. It's Colonial Security after her. Colonial Security. If we bring her to the house, we draw them to us."

He's afraid. Not like me. I know now we can beat them.

I straighten my jacket and continue walking.

"The dark lords of Hell, Dyle," he's saying. "You really want that? We don't have softguns. We don't have any way to protect ourselves."

The street sign. Divine Mercy. I quicken my pace. The skin on my arms, on my chest, freezes. The door to Tal Hendrix's building is propped open. A tenant who forgot his code?

The roster. Check the roster. Too many names. Damn it. Too slow. Then: Hendrix, 1012.

"Dyle?"

I jump into the lift. Beagle gets in with me. The tenth floor hallway's bright. Like the Meat Market. Like . . . I palm the buzzer to 1012 and the outside camera swings my way.

The door opens. She's still alive.

"There's been a murder," I tell her.

"I know."

We walk inside. The place is huge. A household bot is recharging at the wall socket. The place is lush with plants.

"I want you to come with us."

"For questioning?"

"Pack your things, Mrs. Hendrix. Please pack them now."

She looks at the expensive furniture, the statuary, as if overwhelmed by the chore. Without another word, she walks to the bedroom.

I take a seat on the couch. Beagle sits next to me. "I thought the government took all her money. How'd she get these things? And how'd she find out about the murder?''

Then she's walking out of the bedroom, toting two suitcases. Already packed. Someone's been giving her money. Someone warned her. Where was she planning to hide?

Beagle takes the suitcases. I go to the kitchen, palm the cabinets open. Silverware. Ladles. Knives.

Eight inch blade. I slide it into my jacket. A small one for her, like the illegal knife that . . . three inches. A woman's weapon.

I walk back into the living room. Beagle and Mrs. Hendrix are staring at me. I go to the bot. Unfasten two extension arms. Heft the metal tubes for weight. Not too heavy. Not flimsy.

I put the tubes down. Stand before her, face to face. "The knife is your last line of defense." Pick up her hand. Put the knife in it. "Hold it like this. You have more strength that way."

"Dyle. Stop scaring her."

"She's not scared." Eyes. Not warm brown. Not soft brown. Resilient. And very still. They remind me of something. "Put it in your pocket." She obeys.

I take her hand again. Small, but not fragile. I fold it gently into a fist. "Here." I place it low on my belly. A tingle. And my skin fevers at her touch. "If he comes at you, here's where you put the knife. Don't stab. Slide it in, then bring the blade up fast." Navel. Stomach. Bottom of my sternum. "Don't go for the heart. You'll hit bone. You have to go for the soft tissue."

The look she gives me, like . . . that time at the zoo.

Cages of big cats. A man walking between the guardrail and the bars. Past sleeping tigers. Indolent lions. And in the last cage, two leopards looked up from their nap.

"Kill him," I tell her. "You'll have to kill him."

I slide her hot fist around my belly. It leaves a burning trail across my side. "If he grabs you, go for the kidneys." Warm stomach to warm stomach. Breasts against my chest.

But I release her. Stand back. Pick up the tube. "This is your first defense. Don't go for the head. He'll duck. Women think you should go for the testicles, but men expect that. They're used to defending themselves there."

That sharp attention. Like a leopard's.

"On the side of the thigh." I steady her with one hand and tap her thigh lightly with the tube. I feel her knee crumple. Feel her catch herself before she can fall. "No matter how big he is, he'll go down. And when he does, he'll fall to the side and forward." I fold her fingers around the tube. Lift her wrist. "Just below the skull. That's where you hit him." The tube is cold against my neck. Wrist hot in my hand.

"Don't run." She won't. Not her. "Don't leave him behind alive." I drop my gaze from watchful eyes to mouth. Rapid pulse at her throat. Not fear. Excitement.

I step back and her eyes track me.

"Let's go," Beagle says. "We need to talk to Pearcy."

Pearcy. I've forgotten.

"Come on. Come on. Let's go." Beagle picks up the suitcases and walks out the door.

When we reach the street, I notice how she walks. Long, loose strides. Head up. Alert. Like Lila. When the man walked near their cage, the leopards went alert like that.

"You have to listen for every sound," I tell her. Beagle's heavy footsteps. Hers light.

She taps the tube against her leg. Feeling for that nerve. That sweet spot. Remembering.

"Always know who or what's behind you. Know what's up ahead. If he comes after you, don't run. Face him. Always face him."

She flicks the hair off her forehead. Tawny hair. Her eyes move back and forth as if she can see in the dark.

"Don't ever let him get the knife away from you." Lila's mistake. "He'll use it on you. Promise me. Promise."

Did she notice the pain in my voice? Her eyes flick to me. Then away.

I swallow hard.

He Shall Reign is closer than I thought. At Pearcy's place we stop.

"You stay here," I tell Beagle. "I'll go get Pearcy and I'll take Mrs. Hendrix with me. Always check the lift," I tell her. I look in. Empty. We squeeze inside. When the lift stops we get out, and she looks both ways.

I halt at the entrance to Pearcy's apartment. "Stay out here. Keep your back to the wall."

She's eyeing the corridor, the closed doors.

I push aside the curtain and go in. The mattress has been moved. Dragged to the other side of the room. In the square glow from the window, I see Pearcy's legs.

"Pearcy?"

Doesn't answer. Maybe passed out drunk. I walk to him. Put my hand out.

Something's wrong.

All wrong. Empty eye sockets ooze. His mouth is open, the clapper of his tongue gone.

I stumble into something. Reece? Just a table. It upends with a crash. The dog in apartment eleven starts to bark.

"Major?"

Her. Tal. Not . . . I push back the curtain.

"Major?" Voice hushed.

"Get out of here. Get on the lift. Tell Beagle."

"But—"

"Do it now!"

Could still be around. Of course he is. Hiding. Listening. Thinks he'll get to me. Thinks I'll scream. Thinks—

"Goddamn it! Go get Beagle!"

She starts toward the lift. It opens.

"Check it first! Check it!"

I lunge to her. Drag her back. Check the lift myself. It's empty. Push her in. Hit the DOWN button. And she's gone. Safe.

Go back to Pearcy's apartment. Won't look at the body. Won't give Reece the satisfaction. Learned that lesson. Learned it well. He's not hiding in the closet. Not in the kitchen.

The clank of the lift. I stiffen. Footsteps in the corridor. I slip past the curtain again. Ready. Tube upraised. Just Beagle. Just Tal Hendrix.

"He killed Pearcy. Check all the apartments." I pound on the nearest door. Apartment nine. The old lady. "Police! Open up! It's the police!''

The tube leaves a dent in the door.

"Dyle?" Beagle's walking out of Pearcy's apartment. "Come on, Dyle. Let's go."

Apartment eleven. I hit the door so hard it trembles in its frame. The dog inside barks. I hit it again. Harder. Harder. A shiver through the metal. Tingle in my hands. Can't hold on. And the tube goes flying.

"Dyle, don't—"

I push him away. "Shut up, goddamn it."

If Kanz had just shut up. If he hadn't spoken. Hadn't said her name.

I rub my eyes. Sticky warmth down my cheeks. Rub them to dig memory out. Dark purple flowers. Comets of bright. The skin on my eyes is so hot it burns.

Someone—Beagle—seizes my wrists. "Don't."

Just can't hold on any longer.

"Look at me, Dyle. Look."

I can't.

"Open your eyes. Come on."

Tal says, "God. Why did he do that? Why did he hurt himself like that?"

Sticky. All over me. My eyes hurt. I open them. Red. All around, red.

"Let's get out of here," Beagle says.

He releases my wrists. My eyes are on fire. There's red on my hands. Bloody skin under my nails.

28

We walk in the house. Szabo's sitting on the sofa. He looks at Tal Hendrix. At my bloody face. "It's started. Hasn't it."

"What?" Beagle asks.

"The bad things. I'm not much of a clairvoyant, but I sense—are you going to send me home?"

Beagle tells him, "Dyle says we won't send you home unless you want to go."

"Thanks. I appreciate that. But I won't touch things anymore. Milos told me to be careful. Said death comes through doors."

"Yeah, fine. Let's go to bed," Beagle says. "I'll give you a trank."

Szabo doesn't get up. "You're Paulie Hendrix's widow, aren't you. You'll excuse me for not shaking hands. Sensitized, you see. The psychometry has me sensitized, and my hands are raw." His hands curl in his lap as if the palms have been scalded. "It's not that I want to be impolite, but I don't like looking into people."

"Come on, goddamn it," Beagle says. "Go to bed."

Szabo gets up and shuffles to his room, leaving waves of silence in his wake.

Beagle grabs Mrs. Hendrix's suitcases. "I'll show you where you can stay," he says. They walk down the hall. I go to my own room, pull off my bloody shirt and study myself in the mirror.

Across my eyelids are ploughed angry rows. Purple bruises blossom between the furrows. I shower, slip on a clean pair of shorts, and walk out of the bathroom. Beagle's seated on my bed.

"Someone needs to take a look at those scratches." He holds up a tube of Dermagro.

I stretch out on the comforter. Beagle moves the lamp closer, squeezes cream on his fingers. "Szabo's crazy. Didn't I tell you? This whole thing's going to fall apart. And you're getting careless. That goes against your grain, being careless. You hate that in people."

He rubs cream in my eye. It stings. I jerk my head away.

But he catches my chin in his strong fingers. Forces me still. "One of your pet peeves, in fact. Carelessness. There's not much empathy for victims in your psychological profiles. Not much at all."

Cream on my lips. Tastes like rancid milk. "Leave me the hell alone, Beagle."

"Just hold still. Christ. You made a mess out of yourself. You're making a mess out of everything."

I open my eyes. Beagle's putting the top on the tube of cream.

I tell him, "Don't get between me and Tal Hendrix." I'd kill him if he tried.

He knows. He gets up. The bed rebounds. He wipes his hands on his slacks.

"A mess, Dyle. A fucking mess."

He leaves and I close my eyes.

Someone's screaming, faint and far away. I'm in Chicago East Prison. A shadowy mausoleum of a place. I move down the peeling hall. Beagle's behind me, talking about women. Szabo is opening doors.

Don't open that—I say. Too late. The door slides open. Inside the room is a heap of rust-stained clothes.

Heart pounding, I pivot, come face to face with Beagle. Fuck 'em till they scream—he says.

We travel down, down into the viscera of the prison. In a mildewed holding cell seepage stands ankle-deep. A monster's in the basement. I know it. It's always been there.

The kitchen. Everything will be all right if we can just get to the kitchen. I tug on Beagle's arm, trying to get him to leave.

Slick juicy cunts—he says and smacks his lips.

No one wants to go to the kitchen, and I can't go alone. Steep steps now. Narrow steps. Arched ceiling. Everything painted verdigris green. A light shines up from the bottom, reflects against lumpy, careless paint.

Can we go back now?—

Szabo doesn't hear me. At the bottom of the stairs is a door.

Don't open that!—

But Szabo has his hand on the knob.

Oh, please. For Christ's sake, Szabo. Don't open that!—

Szabo turns, a wide insane grin on his face. My breath catches in my throat. The door opens. The darkness behind is chill. I smell the stench of something fetid, of something that has been left a long time in the earth.

Milos Arne is standing there.

29

I wake up, arms flailing. Catch my breath, and let my heart slow. Dreaming. Did I make a sound? No one comes to see. I watch sun track a path up the mounded covers.

The scent of coffee lures me from bed. I check my face in the mirror. The swelling is down. The Slimcast is blue. I peel it off and flush it. Electrodes have left a series of dirty circles across my ribs that don't come off in the shower.

I dry off, pull a uniform from the Wash & Press, and walk into the kitchen. Tal Hendrix is sitting at the table. Her presence stuns me.

"Hello, Major. I made coffee. Can I get you a cup?" She starts to get to her feet.

"No."

Silence as I take down a mug and pour my coffee. It's a good silence. A comfortable, homey one. "Are you angry?" she asks.

"No. Why?"

"You snapped my head off just now. Bad night?"

I turn. Did she hear me cry out in my sleep? "Don't ever get coffee for anyone. Not for me. Not for Beagle.

We're not goddamned Tennysonians."

"All right. Fine. I just thought—Well, how's your face feeling?"

I put my hand to my cheek. Ashamed. How she saw me. Weak.

"Beagle told me about your wife. I'm sorry. It must have been terrible, seeing—"

"Yes." Her presence makes the room too hot. I can't breathe. A tingle where her eyes touch me. "Where's Beagle?"

"On the patio."

I walk quickly out of the room, and find I can breathe again.

Beagle is sitting outside in the shade of the overhang. Szabo is up, dressed and standing ankle-deep in the purple groundcover, feeding squirrels.

I sit at the patio table and sip my coffee. Squirrels, eager for food, make a semicircle around Szabo, a cautious distance of about two feet. A miniature no-man's land.

Tal Hendrix in my kitchen. A short walk away. I could go back in there, if I wanted to.

"You feel up to a little excursion?" Beagle asks. "I tracked Greel Iovinelli's partner to Gilead. Thought we should talk to him."

Greel Iovinelli's partner in Gilead. But Tal Hendrix in my kitchen. "I think someone should stay here and keep an eye on things."

"For the Hendrix woman? Szabo's up and around now. You can leave her with Szabo. He won't seduce her." Beagle's arms are crossed over his barrel chest. Between us stands a barren space like that between Szabo and the squirrels.

"I'm not worried about that. I'm worried about Colonial Security. About Vanderslice. About her goddamned safety."

"I thought you gave her a self-defense lesson. Interesting. Sort of a foreplay thing, right? Why don't you let her in on your interrogation techniques next? You could slam her around a little. You could—"

"Shut the fuck up!" Half rise to my feet. Hands clenched. I want to slam my fist into his face. No use. No nerves. Metal underneath. Never loved. Never contemplated suicide. Nothing can hurt Beagle.

"Look, Dyle. You're the big-shot interrogator. I need you on this. I'm just a numbers cruncher. I can't read people as well as you do."

But what if I came home and found her like Pearcy?

"It's not an overnighter. They'll be okay here alone for a few hours."

"I'll be all right."

That voice. I turn. She's standing in the open patio door. How much did she hear?

"I have people looking after me. Go on. Take your trip."

Who? Who looks after her?

"Well, that's settled." Beagle gets to his feet. "I'll call a cab." He walks around her into the house, and we're alone.

I turn quickly. Look at Szabo.

"Don't you want anything to eat before you go?"

I shake my head. Look at my coffee. Feel her eyes on

CONSCIENCE OF THE BEAGLE

me. "Where were you going last night?" I ask.

She doesn't answer.

"When we got to your apartment, you were already packed. Who told you about the murder? Where did you plan to go?"

"Is this an interrogation?" she laughs. "Are you going to slam me around?"

No bone, no metal barrier, to stop it.

"Sorry." Her eyes lower. "The revolutionaries take care of me. I thought I explained that."

I wanted her to need me. "No. You never did."

"They're just some friends of mine. And Paulie's. They're careful. Don't worry. They know what they're doing."

Secret little meetings. They know what they're doing. Who's lying? Vanderslice or her?

Beagle's suddenly in the doorway, just behind her. "Cab's here, Dyle."

I get up. Stop at her shoulder. By the smell of her perfume, the heat of her skin. "You're sure you'll be all right?"

"I'm sure."

A blue cab is waiting. Like the one that melted during the bombing. We get in. The ride to the port is silent.

Still silent, we buy our tickets. We file onto the plane and take our seats. I say, "If you want control of the team, just tell me."

The doors close. The steward walks quickly to the back of the cabin. A restraint lowers over my lap. Over Beagle's. Metallic clicks as they lock.

Beagle stares out the window. Gray tarmac flashes by.

WARNING. WARNING. TAKE OFF MODE. Foot-high red letters on the wall. A bang from the rear of the cabin and the plane shudders. Gravity sits on my lap.

"I don't give a shit about who gives the orders. It doesn't matter anymore." By Beagle, a window. In it, a divided world: the blue of Tennyson's atmosphere; the black of space.

He looks out.

"What do you want from me, damn it?"

"A little help might be nice. I didn't lose my wife. I didn't lose my former lover. But I'll tell you something . . ." He turns. Behind him, blinding white cloud and cobalt ocean. "You're fucking up the case, Dyle."

I start to say—What? Then the plane is buffeting in for a landing. A moment later, we're down.

When the restraints release, Beagle is on his feet. I rise and follow.

It's raining in Gilead, a dismal, slow rain. The air smells of the sea. Beagle dodges a luggage carrier. He selects a red cab from the gaily-colored loaves at the front of the port. We get in. He gives it Greel Iovinelli's address.

Gilead is a tourist trap with blocks and blocks of shops. We pass people lunching under a canopy. The cab climbs the shoulder of a green mountain, slows and rolls to a stop. Beagle slips his card through the reader. The doors open.

The office is a glass box perched on the side of the hill. Below it are black wet rocks and turbulent sea. Beagle rings the buzzer. A young man opens the door. He has on a pair of yellow shorts. A purple shirt open to the waist. His blond hair stands up in odd spikes around his head. There's a squeegee in his hand.

"Mr. Piper?" Beagle asks.

"Hey." He flashes a dim-wittedly cheerful smile. He looks at my face and his grin wavers. Questioningly, he turns to Beagle.

"I called you this morning about the death of your partner, Greel Iovinelli?"

The smile dims. "Yeah. What a rooter, Greel slipping out like that. Get in, okay?" And he steps away from the door.

He leads us to his workstation room. Walls of glass. Great view of the ocean.

Beagle tells him so.

Piper nods. "I don't know if I can keep up the payments on this place now. Such a rooter, but what can you do?" Then Piper brightens. "Hey. Mind if I keep working? Got a deadline."

"Go ahead," Beagle says.

Piper sits at his screen and applies the squeegee to the screen. He's building a bookcover for something called *The Ascension Murders*. A greenish body lies in the foreground, half in, half out of an alley. It's surrounded by a pool of cherry red blood.

I look quickly away. "How well did you know Paulie Hendrix?" I ask.

Piper lifts his unoccupied left hand, presses the first and second fingers together. "Glued. I did most of his artwork."

"But Greel was working on something for him when he was killed."

He bobs his head. Drops the squeegee. Runs his hands through his hair, leaving the greasy blond strands on end. Then he recovers from his artistic fit and picks up the squeegee again.

He punches in a darker red, starts working on the shadows. "Had another assignment. Paulie called me at the last minute, and, hey, a rooter, but I was deadlined. I asked Greel if he could handle it. He got the commission. *Godly Science* didn't pay well, but they always paid on time. Somebody's going to get a lot of neg-E for slipping out Paulie."

"Can we see what Greel was working on?" I ask.

Without lifting the squeegee from the screen, Piper jerks his head toward the neighboring unit. "Log on WINTERIZE. Check in the directory under GS."

I one-handedly tap out the logon. I wait.

Gray rain drums the windows. On the far wall is a flat painting of a man and a woman on a beach, drinks in their hands, hats pulled over their eyes. They look either very relaxed or asleep. Under the picture the words: WINTERIZE ME.

I ask for the directory. Find GS. Hit enter. And study the screen. "It's not here."

Piper looks up. "Should be. We download from the master. The original always stays with us."

"There's an entry for GS in the directory, but no data."

He gets up. Looks at the screen himself.

"Any way that could have happened accidentally?"

"Not that I know of."

"What was Greel working on?"

"I don't know. Hey. I don't do science. Paulie just gave me the specs and I filled them in. Greel worked that way, too."

"Did Greel Iovinelli know John Vanderslice?"

Piper looks glumly into the drizzle. Below us waves hurl themselves against the rocks. "Greel and I were on the list."

"What list?"

"The *list*. You know. Of subversives. Greel wrote this bump-and-grind article about Vanderslice in *Journal of Art*. Greel told me he walked up to him at an exhibition once and tried to introduce himself. He told him what hole he could fill." He returns to his work as if real mysteries don't interest him.

Beagle asks, "Have you ever met Vanderslice?"

"No. Hey. But I'd like to tell him what hole he could fill, too." Piper leans back. Studies his handiwork.

"Why'd you do the corpse that color?" I ask.

"Rotting, you know?"

"Dead bodies are pale. They're sort of colorless. And in the shadows blood looks black."

He turns. "It's a bookcover. Got to have color."

"When the blood pools at the point of lividity, the rest of the body turns dingy yellow."

"You sure?"

"You ever see a corpse?"

"No."

Cold pale wax. What's left when the blush on the cheeks is gone. And it was like I didn't know her anymore. ''Dead bodies are dingy yellow.''

Piper's hair has begun to sag. He pulls at it until it's standing on end. He stares in dismay at the nearly-completed screen. ''Rooter,'' he says.

30

On the ride back from the port I tell Beagle, "Everything's coming to a head. We've got to have a meeting with Marvin."

"Crap. And show him what, Dyle? What proof do we have?"

"We don't need proof. We can tell him what we suspect."

"Unzip your pants, for Christ's sake. Your brain needs air."

Rain clouds have sailed to Hebron and set anchor. The trunks of the pines are damp black, the needles brilliant green.

"Vanderslice is going to assassinate him, Beagle. He's going to make us look like assholes."

"Destiny will make us assholes." He hits the window release. The cab fights a small war with him. Beagle wins by hitting the override button. Cool air and an aerosol of rain wash into the cab.

"How long do we have, you think, before the Chosen's assassinated?" I ask.

"If he's going to be hit, and that's starting to look like

a big if, we have a little time. Otherwise they wouldn't have bothered trying to get rid of us.''

''Why a big if?''

He shrugs.

''The God's Warriors have to have explosives somewhere.''

Beagle stares at the rain, the green lawns, the houses. ''A division of the God's Warriors is in charge of road building and maintenance.''

''That's it, then. Maybe Marvin visits the Division of Highways and the building goes up. Let's check his itinerary.''

''Look. I'm not sure anymore if Vanderslice has anything to do with this. The scenario has the counterfeit feel of a Tennyson blow job. Vanderslice wouldn't have to kill Marvin. He could just leak enough about his insanity to politically drown him.''

''But what about the planted conspiracy angle? He's guilty. We can prove that. No one else could get into those DEEPs.''

''Don't be too sure. Besides, I'm afraid we have a no-winner anyway. Even if Vanderslice is implicated, Marvin wouldn't move against him. Don't you imagine Vanderslice has a file on Fat Boy? Wouldn't you like to know what's in it?''

''But—''

''But we don't know enough yet to tell the Chosen anything. That's that.''

The cab stops in front of the neo-adobe. ''What if you're wrong? What if Vanderslice is cleverer than you think he is? What if he's managed to fool you?''

"Dyle. Nobody's that clever." Beagle climbs out of the cab. Leaves me to pay.

I follow Beagle to the door. Tal Hendrix greets us. Tells us she has dinner waiting.

I go wash up. I'm the last to enter the dining room. One empty chair, and it's next to her. I sit down next to the heat of her body. Watch how her fingers fold over the handle of the knife.

Szabo takes a bite of spinach. Stares into his plate. "Corpses aren't green."

My fork drops. Ziti and carrot slices spill over the table.

Szabo's eyes are wide. "I don't know why I said that."

"Endwrapping," I say. "Damn, you guys get weird when you start endwrapping. You're not going to be doing a lot of this, are you?"

"I see flashes of things, but I can't tell whether they're from the past or the future. Milos comes and goes a lot. An old woman is standing by the sink." He points to empty space. "See her?"

"Szabo. Stop it. There's nothing the hell there."

"I've been seeing a lot of dead people lately. Something terrible is going to happen."

Angry now. And fearful. I push my plate away.

"Remember the time Mars' Helena colony blew out?" Szabo looks around the table. Tal Hendrix isn't eating. Beagle chases a ziti with his fork.

"I saw it. I heard the screaming. I told HF, too. But a psychic only sees so much. I couldn't tell them when. Couldn't tell them where. Three days later the dome went. That's when I understood why the ground I saw in my vision was red." Szabo cuts a square of steak and leaves it sitting, a cubic mountain, on the white plain of his plate. "It's like that now. Just pictures. You and Beagle and a lot of darkness. That's all I know."

Tal gets up. Leaves the bot to clear her plate. Beagle shoves away from the table casually as if he's on his way to the couch and a program on the vid.

I tell Szabo, "I don't want to hear about it."

"Milos says you have to."

I leave. Go to my room.

In the bath, I take off my shirt. Wash my face. When I walk into the bedroom, Tal is standing there.

She holds up a tube of Dermagro. "You need to put some of this on."

"All right."

She looks at me doubtfully. Then at the tube. "You really need to put this on. It'll take the rest of the swelling down."

Swelling already, and we're not even touching. Telltale twitch in my pants.

"You're not going to, are you, Major. I can tell. You're hard-headed."

Hard. Hope she doesn't notice. "I'll be fine."

She opens the tube. Puts ointment on her fingers. Comes over and grabs my wrist. Strong grip. Strong for a woman. I turn, but she pulls me around. Nearly stumble. Facing her now. So close. The scent of her perfume. Her hair.

She lifts her hand to my face. I jerk back. "Don't." Don't deserve her concern. God. Don't want her pity.

I back away, around a chair, the bed. She follows, laughing at me. A low chuckle in the back of her throat.

I'm startled. Hurt. And then—all of a sudden it's so funny.

Stumble over my feet and I'm falling backward. Twist of my body, and my hand hits the carpet first. She falls on top, warm, straddling me. Straddling me, but—

Sharp thing against my bare stomach. She isn't laughing anymore.

"Slide the knife up," she says. "Isn't that right?"

Afraid to breathe. Point barely grazing my skin. Her watchful eyes. Keen eyes. Like the leopards'.

"But what happens if I slice down?"

Down. Down. Stomach. Navel. Not cutting. Doesn't hurt really. It feels—a fingernail. That's what it is.

Lingers for a moment at the top of my pants. I know she can feel how hard I am. Just cloth between us, and I'm hard enough to split the seams.

A flick of her fingers. My pants' clasp parts. Down. Excruciatingly slow. Spreads the smooth edges of the zipper.

And she halts. Just the edge of her finger.

She moves fast. Gets up to leave. Going away, up and over the bed. I seize her ankle. Her shoe drops off, and I climb her. Legs. Ass. Her pants slip. Pale skin. Pink heat underneath. Dimple at the top of her buttocks. Fighting. What if she's not playing?

Slaps me. My ribs. Slaps hard. Trying to sit up. I straddle her this time. Thin cloth between us. She's strong, but I'm stronger.

Pants around her hips from our struggle. Line of curly blond hair. Darker than on her head. Just a shade darker. Like—

But her eyes are brown. And wide. Scared. Or is she? What if she wants me to stop?

Fingernails rake my hips, pull my slacks—Oh, Christ— the rest of the way. I spring out so hard I wonder how the cloth contained it. The room's hot. So hot I've started to tremble. She's kicking her pants off now. Pulling off her sweater. She's frantic for it. Heel of her foot bruises my leg.

Breasts larger than Lila's. I put my hand there. She knocks it away. But Lila—she grabs me. Squeezes. Please, tighter. And her hand moves. Up and down. Have to hold it in. Not this soon. Then her head lowers against my stomach. Tickle of silky hair. My hips strain. Strain for her mouth. Want to let go, but can't have her like that. Not faceless.

Push her against the bed. Her eyes fly open. Brown. Have to remember that her eyes are brown. Her breasts so large. Nipples puckered and pink. Find the spot. Find it blind. She's tighter than I thought. So tight that waiting aches. It'll all get away from me. Ruin it for her. And I want it to be perfect.

She doesn't understand why I stopped. Shoves me into her, like she wants everything I have. Like she wants more.

Legs clasp my ass. Burning tracks on my back from her nails. She wants me so bad.

Christ. Can't hold on anymore. Plunge into her violent and quick. She shivers like there's cold steel in her, not flesh. Her smell. Sweat and perfume and the sea. God. A dark rush coming. Drive so deep my muscles lock. A pump, the first one easy. The second quivers up my thighs, shoots into the base of my groin. Powerful as the explosion of the bus. She shivers. Shivers. Her body goes so limp that for a moment—afraid. What did I—

Then she sighs and everything's all right. Everything's okay. I kiss the rapid pulse at her throat. Lay my head on the slick sweated skin between her neck and shoulder. Breathing in gasps. We both are. I could lie like this all night, inside her. Go to sleep like this. Just the two of us.

She moves. Limp now. I slide out and fall away. Want the comfort back. Like safety. That's what it's like. Just knowing she's there. If I was hard again . . . but no, she's so tired. Wouldn't bother her like that. Don't think I even could. Just want to lie inside.

She inches out from under me and rolls over, stopped by the tether of my arm. Won't she tell me how good it was? At the base of her skull her hair is damp. I kiss behind her ear. The back of her neck. Taste salt sweat and bitter dregs of perfume. Her eyes are closed. Her mouth is parted, breathing.

Never loved him. And he never loved her. Only someone who cherishes could love like I just did. Didn't she feel it? So tender, really, in a way. Like the leopards.

I slip my arm around the mound of her belly and close my eyes and see the leap of the cats. Remember how my heart leaped too, and I shouted a warning. But the man at the cage ignored me. The leopards pounced. Pounced. And pushed their heads against the bars until he scratched behind their ears. Greedy for affection. *It's all right*, the man told me. *I'm their vet.*

Claws and teeth. They could have torn him apart, but they didn't. She let me love her like that.

Won't she tell me how good it was? But it must have been, because she's already asleep. I put my ear to her bare shoulder and hear the pump of her heart. I pull the blankets up around her and she stirs a little. Careful not to wake her.

Paulie Hendrix never loved her like I did. I gently lift her damp hair from her shoulders and spread it out on the pillow.

My arm wants to stay. Wants to hold her there—at the bars. In the cage. But I get out of bed. My back burns where she scratched me. I pull my slacks on and walk out the door.

Look back once. Asleep in the glow of the lamp. Face relaxed. Mouth barely parted. Claws sheathed. I close the door and go to the living room.

Beagle's not there, but his workstation is up. I punch in the Hendrix file and read. There. A picture. So old. Thank God. So old. Weak bland eyes. Bland face. Paulie Hendrix never loved her like I did.

Hungry all of a sudden. I go to the kitchen, grab a box—the shrimp—from the pantry and put it in the oven. While it's heating, I get cheese out of the refrigerator and bite right into the block. Crackers next. Onion flavored. Only after half the package do I wonder if she'll smell it on my breath.

A sound. I turn. Beagle's standing in the doorway.

The oven blats. I pull my dinner out, rip the package apart. Crisp breading. Sweet meat inside. When I turn again, he's still watching me, disapproving.

"You need to put something on those scratches, Dyle. Your back's a mess."

I eat. I eat. When I look up again, he's gone.

31

I wake up with my arm around her. Belly to warm back. Legs entwined. I put my head against her neck, breathe in her smell: sweat and a woman smell of satiation. She's still asleep. I'm hard again, but can't wake her. I remember how Lila hated that.

Everything's changed. Just this morning. Like opening a door into another, brighter room. Did she feel it? All those years with Paulie. Better than him. Those bland eyes. Still . . .

Wasn't in complete control. Could have made it better for her. But couldn't help myself. She's more than the expensive whores after Lila. So much more that it scares me. With the whores it was mechanical. But I'd have them, anyway. And then I'd go home and try to capture Lila with my hand. This time . . .

Wish she'd wake up. Slow, even breaths. Eyes closed. I wait for her to stir. She doesn't. Quietly I get out of bed, put on my slacks. Coffee. She'll want coffee.

I leave the room. The kitchen is empty. I set the coffee to brew. Cream? Sugar? How does she like it? Everything has to be perfect.

I want her so bad my hand shakes. Fill a mug. Heat a Danish. Blueberry. Hope she likes it. When I take the plate and mug to the room, she's still asleep. I set her breakfast on the end table where she'll see it. So she'll know how I . . .

Can't leave her. Can't wake her up. I go in the bathroom, brush my teeth, take a shower. While I'm scrubbing, I see a pink form through the frosted glass.

Turn off the water. Slide open the partition. She's at the sink, brushing her teeth.

Heavier than Lila. Bigger boned. Lila was whipcord thin. I step out, water dripping. I stand behind her, close enough for her to feel how hard she makes me. I move my damp hands down, down her back, that nip at her waist, rounded buttocks.

I look into the mirror. She's frozen, eyes closed, still holding the toothbrush. I watch my hands slide her belly, her breasts. Soft skin. Woman's skin. She lets the brush fall. Leans against me. I slip between her legs, as if I always belonged there. Secure as a gloved hand.

Pick her up. So gently. Set her on the counter. She's breathing hard. Greedy thighs part. I let her guide me in.

But slow this time. Slow. I bend her backwards and sweep my arm across the counter. Bottles fly. They crash against the partition. Clank when they hit the floor.

Hold her down with one hand. And watch her face. Brown eyes, but that's all right. The expression's like Lila's. Sleepy, nearly.

So slow I can watch it happen. Look at myself in the mirror then. Calm, controlled. Not like her. Her lips look swollen. Her eyes are closed. Strange how such a sleepy face can seem so eager.

She cries out. Not a word. Just a sound, like an animal. Want her to beg like I've begged. No one should have that power.

Expression changes. Mouth slacks. Head arched back against the mirror. Gasping for breath. Feel her insides spasm, grab me. Excited, but I'm still in control. Contained, until I feel her shudder. Feel her thighs jitter against me. See civilization leave her face, all manners, all niceties, all coolness.

Her skin's flushed and hectic pink. She goes limp. But not yet. Won't let her go just yet. I slide one finger over her breast.

She cries out again. Won't she say my name? Just once. Just once.

I whisper hers. "Tal."

I move in the cage of her legs. She doesn't open her eyes. Her whole body strains to me. Toy with her. Just a moment more. And then—

Spurts of release so hard, so fast, they're shocking. Nearly bring tears to my eyes. Tal. Tal. I say her name over and over like the simple cry of an animal.

Her eyes are closed. I want her to open them. To look at me. Want her to say my name. Sweat clings to us like skin. No one ever loved her like this. No one could.

I pull out. Help her up. Hold her. Tight to me. Want her again. This is crazy. Couldn't do anything. Not for a while.

Slumps against my chest. In my arms. Tired and trusting. I whisper her name. It barely disturbs the damp hair near her ear. Want her to tell me she loves me.

But she pushes me away. Not angry. But so firmly I'm startled. She goes to the cabinet and takes out a towel. Turns her back, wipes herself. Wraps the towel around her. Angry? No. Inhibited.

Of course. A Tennysonian. Must have been taught that sex is wrong. Must have been difficult for her, wanting it so bad. Ashamed of it.

Won't hide myself like that. I'll teach her to enjoy things. I run my hand down her arm, reading her skin's texture.

She shies from under my touch and laughs. "You're dangerous, Major. I like that in a man."

How could I be so hot a moment ago, and now be cold? She picks up the toothbrush. Her face in the mirror is civilized. Cool. A little distant.

"Why were you crying?"

She stops brushing. Looks into my reflected eyes. Puzzled. Doesn't remember. But I can't forget.

"When John Vanderslice came to the Meat Market. You were crying. Why?"

Eyes drop. She opens the tap. A hiss of water.

"Did he hurt you?"

"No."

Did he have her? He knows the Meat Market trick. Maybe he wanted more. "What sort of hold does he have on you?"

Eyes resilient as hardwood.

"Don't ever be alone with Vanderslice again."

"Damn it. Don't try to tell me what to do. What right do you have to tell me what to do?"

I have all rights. More than her husband. He never

knew how she wanted. Never watched her face go through
that change. Never made her body shudder with it.

Quietly, "I worry about you, is all."

"I'm not a child, Major."

My name. Please say my name.

"Not even my husband had the right to tell me where
to go. Or who to see."

Cold. I step back. Had affairs. Of course she did.
Couldn't keep that frenzy caged so long. And maybe
someone was better. She likes dangerous men.

Want to wrap my arms around her. Afraid I'll hold ice.
"There's a man here." Catch a glimpse of my own face
in the mirror. I look scared. "A man from Earth's Colonial Security. He's working with Vanderslice. But he's out
of control."

Like she was this morning. Like I was last night. I
understand the man's mind. Know he can't stop because
murder feels too good.

Her full attention. Not frightened, but sees the panic in
me.

"He has a softgun."

Rinses out her mouth. Turns off the tap. "The people
guarding me have softguns."

"But not like this."

That keen regard. So sharp it hurts.

"He likes to kill. He's good at it. I know Colonial
Security. I know how they are. Your people won't have
a chance."

Shrugs. Damn her. She shrugs.

"He's too good. Has Vanderslice scared now. Even
Vanderslice. And you know what a son of a bitch he is.

That's how good this man is. Even Vanderslice can't stop him.''

Want to scare her bad. So she'll turn to me. So she'll need me.

"Wet work. That's what Colonial Security is good at. Assassinations. Murders. That's why the man is here. Earth sent him to help Vanderslice become the Chosen. To get rid of Marvin. That's the plan. This man killed your husband. Don't you understand? Probably killed him just to shake Vanderslice up. To show him who's the boss—''

She turns away. Bends down to start the shower. The towel rides up. All that's left of our lovemaking is the red indentation across her ass. But still, I had her.

"They're going to assassinate Marvin. Didn't you hear?''

Over the drumming of the water, her even, bland words, "Don't be ridiculous.''

I grab her. Her body's stiff. She pulls away from me. "You're in danger,'' I say. "He's after me. He'll kill you to get to me. He wants—''

She says, "If you're so worried about that, I can leave. Hide somewhere else.''

God. No. No. Does she think someone can protect her better? Love her better? "He'll find you. Colonial Security's too good. You never hide well enough. I have to tell Marvin. Maybe he can stop it. He can cut off diplomatic relations—''

She slaps me hard in the chest. Drives me backward a pace. And I want her so bad I hurt.

"Tennyson is a prison, damn it! Don't you see that?

Are you blind or what? Let them kill Marvin if they want to."

"God, Tal. Listen to me. Earth will take over."

"So? It can't be any worse."

"Yes, it can. It can. You don't know—" Doesn't know how dark Earth is. How far from the light.

"There's a contact high up in the government. I'll warn him."

"That's not enough." Nothing's enough.

"You can't talk to Marvin, Major. Everything's on the edge."

Call me by my name, damn you. My name. I'm on the edge. At the brink.

"Give me some time," she says. "If you talk, you'll ruin everything."

But she's ruined it already. Why is she cold? Did I say—did I do something wrong? I take a clean uniform from the Wash & Press. I stalk out of the bedroom and dress. Leave her to shower alone.

I go to the kitchen, get a cup of coffee, and take it outside. Beagle is sitting at the patio table watching Szabo feed the squirrels.

His gray eyes pick me apart. "How are you feeling?"

"Fine."

"You sure?"

"Of course I'm sure."

"Because I heard interesting noises coming from your room last night. And—a bit lively, aren't you? Seems I heard them again this morning. You look depressed. Why?"

The cup pauses at my lips. "None of your fucking business."

"Right now your fucking is my business, Dyle. It's my business. It's Szabo's. It's Vanderslice's. It's Marvin's."

I push the cup away. Sun on Beagle's cheek turns the mock skin pink as if blood flows there. What a marvel he is, really. How carefully crafted. Each hair. Each pore. He sits forward, lacing those perfect fingers. "There's something I have to tell you."

His gaze is intent. Pained. Like Kanz's. "About two years ago Szabo began endwrapping. HF sent him to a counselor. Gave him a desk job."

Szabo. An enigmatic St. Francis. Stopped feeding the squirrels. He's looking across the purple yard to the table. Squirrels gather faithfully at his feet.

"He was living with Milos Arne then."

Suddenly Tal opens the patio door. She's holding a mug of coffee. The mug I brought her. Beagle shoots her a warning glance. She doesn't sit down.

"Arne was always a problem. You can guess that, I think. He was working with a woman, Hiko Black. They hated each other. A few months later a promotion came up. Arne had more seniority, but the woman got the promotion. And Arne was demoted."

Beagle's gaze is so still. Apologetic.

"Hiko Black rode Arne unmercifully. Arne couldn't do anything right. About the same time Szabo was put back in service."

Beagle's scrutiny. It strips the skin from my face, leaves me exposed to the air.

"They gave him the Mahoud case."

Mahoud. Level 6. Sweet, elderly man on a pension. He explained to the arresting officers in his pleasant, patient way how much he disliked vat-grown meat. Which was why he lured over twenty children to his apartment.

"The case was torture for Szabo. There were very few clues, but the kids just kept disappearing. Szabo was put on the case at victim seven. He watched the rest of them vanish. That's when he and Milos Arne began to fight."

The yard is empty of squirrels now. Szabo stands alone, sun on his bald head a halo.

"It was a disaster. Arne was demoted. They moved to Level 3 for a while. But Szabo couldn't stand Arne's complaints. He moved out, went back to Level 4 alone." Beagle grabs my arm. "Dyle. I didn't want to have to tell you this."

Bad news coming. I can feel it. Like Szabo and the Helena Colony. Bad news.

"Their lives were ruined. Just like yours was ruined. About eighteen months ago."

The cup clatters to the table. I look at the spilled coffee. How could my hand lose its grip like that?

"Dyle? Didn't you ever wonder why they never caught Lila's murderer?"

"There weren't any clues. That's all. No clues."

"Don't you wonder why Lila went into that alley?"

"She was careless. Just a mistake."

"You know better than that. HF made Szabo an emotional cripple. And Arne loved Szabo. Christ. He loved him until the day he died. You could see it in his face. He never understood why he left. They were together twelve years. Twelve years. Dyle? Don't you see? HF murdered Lila.''

I shove the table into Beagle's chest. "Shut up."

"You have to listen."

Don't.

"Eighteen months ago, HF started blaming me for errors. Stupid errors. Made me question—Christ. Made me crazy. But I was smarter. I found the pattern. Figured it out."

Hurt us where we were the most vulnerable. Szabo's and Arne's love. My love. Beagle's brilliance.

"Eighteen months, Dyle. Just the time Lila died. That Arne was demoted. That Szabo was given the Mahoud case. Just the time the bombings on Tennyson started."

Fumble up from the chair.

"Dyle? I read her file. She was smart and careful. Lila went into that alley with someone she trusted."

Kanz? No, not Kanz.

I push past Tal Hendrix. Blunder through the door. Can't see. Run into Beagle's workstation, nearly knock the table down. The kitchen. Have to get to the kitchen.

"Dyle?" Beagle behind me.

Hit the heel of my hand against a drawer. It pops open. Hit it again. Harder. Harder. Feel the shock of the blows in my shoulder. Silverware jingles.

My mind is sharp. Quick. A small knife. That's what I need. A knife good for getting in tight places.

"What are you doing?" Beagle asks.

I see it. So clearly. Short, sharp blade. Perfect. Slip the knife up my sleeve.

Beagle grabs me and the blade bites.

Kill him. If he doesn't let me go, I'll kill him. Dots of blood on my sleeve. Bright in the glare of the kitchen.

He sees my face. Releases me. "Where are you going with that? What are you going to do?"

"Cut Vanderslice's eyes out."

I turn. He wraps his arm around my neck. Drags me backward. "Get the trank packs out of Szabo's room!" he shouts at Tal. "Go on! Do it now!"

HF killed Lila. Killed her to make Vanderslice Chosen of God. Kanz? Not Kanz. He was crying. I didn't cry. Not me. But maybe Gonzales. His head lowered when he saw me. No. Couldn't have done—None of them could have done that. But he's right. One of them lured her there.

Tal is back. Unbuttoning my sleeve. The knife falls to the floor. Blood-streaked blade. Red runs in a small stream down my arm. Beagle's so strong. I can't—

A slap. The trank pack. My knees go weak. I slump in Beagle's arms. "Kill him," I whisper. Slide down his broad chest to the floor. What's happening? What was I about to do? Oh, that's right. "Cut out his goddamned lying tongue."

32

I lift my head from the pillow. Beagle's standing at the end of the bed.

"Go back to sleep, Dyle. You're still stoned."

Blanket over my feet. Five round bruises on my arm where Beagle held me. Pale square of skin above. The trank patch. I try to sit up. "Where is she?"

"Taking a nap. You wore the woman out this morning. Horny you."

The clock is blinking 4:12. Sunlight is at ebb tide, sucking back from the blinds. The room is beached in sandy-colored glow.

"You knew who killed Lila all the time."

"I've known for a while now, Dyle. Patterns. They're my habitat."

"Earth killed Lila because of him."

"Vanderslice? I'm beginning to doubt it. Although, even if they did, he wouldn't have known."

A bell chimes. Szabo passes the open doorway of my room, shoulders hunched, cadence deliberate and slow.

Beagle looks up, worried. "There's a speaker next to the bell. Why didn't our visitor use it?"

I stumble out of bed. The room swims. Brace myself on the doorjamb, the wall. Shuffle into the kitchen. Vanderslice. In the living room. Duffel bag over his shoulder. Distracted look on his face.

Where's the knife? The goddamned knife? Go to a drawer. Hammer it with my fist. Peelers. Apple corers. Measuring spoons.

Then Beagle grabs me from behind. Pins my arms against my sides.

Vanderslice comes into the kitchen. Looks at me. At Beagle. Crosses to the bot and thumbs the power button. The bot halts, arrested by the sink, can of cleanser in one pincher, sponge in the other.

Vanderslice pulls something from his pocket. Beagle's grip so tight I can't breathe. Remote control. Vanderslice has some sort of remote control.

He points the remote at the window. Faint, flat tink. Like a single note of music. Beagle lets me go.

Vanderslice turns, smiling. "Sexy, huh? This gadget stiffens the glass in the window so the passive ears stationed outside can't pick us up."

Beagle puts a warning hand on my arm.

"The active ears are in the bot. A little trick I picked up at a conference a couple of years ago. Sweepers confuse the bot's signals with the ears' electronics. Can't spot the surveillance worth a damn."

Listening to us all the time. Did he hear what went on in the bedroom? In the bath?

Vanderslice reaches into the duffel bag. Oh, no. He's got a softgun. Hardened the window so no one can hear our screams. Cold spills up my spine. I lunge, but Beagle

stops me. Another softgun. Another. Laying them on the
counter.

"Take it easy, Major. There's one for each of you.
They have your initials on them. Got your fingerprints and
DNA matches from your files, so arming them wasn't
much of a trick. Carry them at all times. Somebody should
stay awake from now on. I guess that would be you, Dr.
Taylor, since you don't need the sleep. Someone slipped
past the body-sound alarm last night. If it hadn't been for
infrared, he would have gotten through."

Surveillance net outside. Got us trapped. Nothing we
can do.

"Who?" Beagle asks.

"We don't know. He had a body muffler. No cardiac
rhythms, no intestinal sounds. Luckily the body heat
soaked through."

"You lying son of a bitch."

Green eyes meet mine.

"Earth killed my wife because of you."

Vanderslice shakes his head. "Okay, Major. I know
what you think. But Earth is after me, too. All of a sudden
this thing has gotten personal and dirty. Harvey Piper was
killed last night with a softgun."

"Rooter," Beagle says.

A bewildered glance. "Anyway, Marv and the council
are giving me these sidelong glances I don't particularly
like. Two softgun murders. And only Internal Safety carries softguns. Don't you see? Dr. Taylor. Come on. Explain it to him, will you?"

"Vanderslice isn't part of it, Dyle. As soon as the
woman was murdered on God's Gift I had that figured

out. Vanderslice wouldn't have been stupid enough to use a softgun.''

He nods. "Okay. So that's understood. I'm going to show you mine now, and I'll want you to show me yours. A tall red-headed man made the Hebron-to-Gilead run at 4:00 in the afternoon, just about the time you were on your way back. He rented a cab at the port, drove over to Piper's house and shot him. Your fingerprints, Major, your sweat, have been found in and around Piper's work area, so I had to step in and keep the Gilead cops from putting out an arrest warrant on you.''

"Now you give us softguns. They can find a murder weapon.''

Vanderslice rolls his eyes. "God, Major. Once you get an idea in your mind, it just gets glued there, doesn't it? I got the Gilead cops to leave you alone because I had a beacon implanted in your ribs during your hospital stay.''

Bastard. Tagged me like a petty thief.

"I knew you were both in Gilead. You were followed to Piper's. If either of you had shot a softgun the beacon would have gone off.''

"Take it out.''

"It's not hurting you or anything, is it? Sometimes they plant them wrong—''

"Get it *out!*''

He's mystified. "You feel really strongly about this, don't you?''

Pulse fast in my temple. I turn. Look at Beagle. "Goddamn it. You knew, didn't you? Knew about Lila. Knew about everything. What the fuck are you pulling? Are you in on it with him?''

"Dyle? Calm—"

"You picked up the signal! You had to."

"No way. I completely fooled him." So proud of himself. "The electrodes on the Slimcast leave a residue. Dr. Taylor would have confused the beacon with that. And I'm not having it taken out. The beacon's so handy, really. Now. Fun's over. I want to know who this red-headed man is. He's not an EPAT. Never been one. So I know he's not ours. He's an Earther."

Beagle nods.

"I've heard you talk about him. Colonial Security, right? But I thought you knew about my surveillance . . ."

Beagle says, "Didn't pick up any signals inside, so . . ."

So brilliant. But never knew.

"Really? No kidding. Great. Wasn't sure what kind of game plan you were following. Whether you were involved. But this morning—well. We're better than I thought, then. That's good. Now. The drunk. Why was Pearcy important enough to be killed? And why did they cut out his eyes? Major? Does the murderer know what happened to your wife?"

Vanderslice knows about Lila. Read my file? No. Heard Beagle and me talking.

"What's going on?"

My breath stops. Tal's voice. Tal in the kitchen doorway. Looking at the guns. At Vanderslice.

He smiles. She comes to him. Don't. Don't. Too close. He could reach out and . . .

Arms fold around one another. His head lowers to her

shoulder. His eyes close and he holds her tight. "God, I missed you."

Missed you. Missed you. The room takes a half-spin to the right. Nothing to stop it. In Vanderslice's face that . . . joy. I should be there, standing in her heat.

Dive for the softguns. Which one, damn it? There. The DH on the butt. It molds to my hand. Senses me. Tingle tells me it's charged. Waited so long. So damned ready.

"Dyle!" Beagle shouts.

Arms drop. They spring apart, guilty. Not sure which one I'll kill until Vanderslice pushes her away.

The barrel follows him. Beagle out of the corner of my eye. Frozen in horror. Nothing can stop me.

Vanderslice. Hands up. Palms out. Not so dangerous now, is he? Is he? He looks toward the door.

Beagle says, "Don't! Don't run. He'll shoot."

Vanderslice goes pale.

"He's part of the revolution," Tal's saying. Voice breathy. "The contact high up in the government. John's the one."

John. Doesn't call me by my name. Not ever. Sweat on my hand. Skin slides on plastic. Sweat on us. Covered both of us.

"Wait a minute. Wait a minute," Vanderslice says. "I get it. But Tal and I—we're just friends." His voice is squeezed, as if I have my hands on his throat. Want to watch him, how softgun victims topple and curl. Fists to chin, trembling. Like she trembled. "Is that what this is all about? We're just friends."

Saw her arms around him. God, her arms were around him. Have him sweat like she sweated. Like she cried out.

"Tal and I . . . We work together, Major. We have for years. Paulie. And Tal. And me."

No.

"Damn you!" Tal screams. "You're messing everything up! It's not John at all! It's not his fault! Earth is behind all this."

Can't hold on. Vanderslice cringes. Hands to his face. He cries out. One syllable.

And I whirl and fire. Shot goes wild. Into the living room. A chair quivers. The armature crackles. Pale stain on the cloth where the material fused.

"Damn it!" Throat raw from my shout. "Goddamn it!" All this time. Never really meant it. Never loved.

I let the gun drop. It clatters against the tiles.

Noise at the door. Banging. Shouts. Three men in suits crash into the room, softguns raised. They look at Vanderslice. At me. At the chair.

"I'm all right," Vanderslice tells them. "Just put the guns away."

Panicked. And out of breath. "We tried to see what was going on, sir. But you were in front of him the whole time. Blocking our view. I tried to get a bead on him—"

"It's all right, Stu."

They put their guns back in their jackets. Look at me again. Shift nervously on their feet.

Vanderslice stands at my shoulder. Awed eyes on the chair. He says weakly, "Good God, Major. You'll never get your rental deposit back."

Tal laughs. He probably always makes her laugh. It was what I loved about Lila, that laughter. And I'm not a happy man. No use. I leave. Leave them all. Go to my bedroom and stare blindly out the window.

Then—tink. Tink.

Vanderslice there behind me, putting away his remote control. "I wanted to talk to you alone."

So sad. The purple lawn abandoned. Empty of Szabo and his squirrels.

"Look at me, Major. Don't speak into the window. This stiffens the glass, but it doesn't insulate sound altogether."

I take a breath. Face him.

"On the south side I was watching Tal every second of every day. After the murder, I called her. Was going to take her to a safe house. But you interfered. Look. I know about your wife. I know how you—well, damn it. You deserve the truth. Tal only went with you, Major . . ." Eyes shift. His. Not mine. So embarrassed he might not finish the thought. Then he says, "because I didn't trust you.

"Hey, look. It's my fault, really. Her idea, though. I shouldn't have told her. Sometimes my mouth just gets away from me. She cried when I said the revolution was failing, and that it was all your fault."

She spied on me.

"So. There you have it." Not embarrassment. Pity.

My face in such tight check that it hurts. Everything hurts.

"No hard feelings? We need each other now. I thought we might get together, you and me. Get to know each other better. Brainstorm a little. Come on over to my house tonight about seven-thirty. My men will pick you up. It's secure and we can talk as long as we like.''

He hikes the duffel bag over his shoulder. He walks to the door. In the hall, he stops. ''Don't bring the softgun.''

33

Can't go back into the living room. Can't look at her.

I stretch out on the bed, close my eyes. So stupid, but I want to hold her again. Nothing else matters. Not the bombings. Not Vanderslice. Nothing.

Lila. At the end of a hall. Dark doors like mouths to either side. Trying to warn me about something. But she's too far. And speaking too softly. I strain to hear. Walk toward her. But she's going. Slipping away.

Oh, stay. Please. Can't you stay with me just for a while?

Mouth moving. But voice so soft. She needs me. Run to help her, but she retreats. Doesn't want to go. She doesn't want to leave me. Who's doing this to us? Who—

Knock at my door wakes me. Beagle.

In the living room, two of Vanderslice's men. And Tal. "Dyle?"

She calls my name. Too late now. Don't look at her. Hurts too much. The men follow me outside.

I get in the limo. Watch shadowy countryside roll by.

Funny, how I thought she loved me.

The car drives between two sniffer gates. Huge sprawling house that looks more grown than built. Like Vanderslice, ostentatious and whimsical. I get out of the limo, walk to the door, and thumb the speaker button. "Major Holloway."

Security camera swings my way. Through the intercom, a congenial, "Come on in."

The massive doors drift apart. I step into an echoing tiled hall.

"This way, Major!" Vanderslice, his voice blunted by distance.

I turn right. Round the corner. Don't know what I expected, but the living room dazes me. Larger than Colonel Yi's. Larger than the one in the Chicago governor's mansion. On a field of peach carpet Vanderslice sits playing with a curly-haired toddler.

"This is Paul. We call him Poo. Say hello, Poo. Say hello to the major."

Paul. A year old. Born about the time of the fourth bombing.

Vanderslice holds the child's wrist. Lifts the arm up and down. Waving. The baby gives me a moronic grin.

Not sure what to do. Never been around children much. Vanderslice looks so natural there. And I'm uncomfortable. I clear my throat.

"Jenny!" Vanderslice calls.

From the depths of the house, a muffled, annoyed answer.

He shrugs. "She's a little busy right now finishing some sort of report. Biologist, you know. Can't get her work published here, but she's well known off-planet. We met at a conference on Stockton. You had dinner yet?''

"No.'' The room is huge, but not austere. Gaily-colored pillows piled in a corner. A wealth of toys. Nanny bot in pink and orange. The air in the room smells of sour milk and talc. A house dominated by a baby. Did Lila ever want this? I wouldn't.

"Come on. I'll get you something to eat.'' He gets up, leaves the toddler with the nanny.

I follow him into the kitchen. "Jenny was too busy to fix dinner tonight, but I have a little of my spiced chicken in the refrigerator. A sandwich all right?''

"Sure.'' The kitchen is huge and bright and cluttered.

"You don't like me much, do you?'' Vanderslice slaps two pieces of bread on a plate. He bends and peers into the refrigerator, waiting for an answer.

An awkward silence. He's too damned young and handsome. Of course I don't like him. He's out of my league.

"And you still don't trust me.'' His voice is pleasant. He lifts a sealpack from the chaos. The refrigerator door slides closed. He moves to the counter. Takes out a knife. But he can't scare me.

He starts slicing a chicken breast. "That's all right. That's okay. It was a long time before I trusted you.'' He eyes me. Then winks. "And I had you under surveillance.''

Tongue between his teeth, he lays slices of meat on the bread. Spoons sauce onto it. "That's why I know . . . this morning. I figured it out when you and Beagle were talking about your wife.''

He turns. Hands the plate to me. His expression is somber. "About Tal . . ."

Won't let him see. "What's in the chicken?"

"Oh. You'll like that. My own recipe. Start off with a real range chicken, one that's scratched for bugs."

Bugs? I look at the sandwich.

"Then you have to marinate it. Can't tell you what's in the sauce, but one of the ingredients is anchovies. Just—will you be careful, Major? Tal's angry about things. Can't blame her, really. She was always a free thinker, and Tennyson doesn't want women to think. How about a beer?"

What does he mean, angry? I'm the one who's angry. Who can't forgive her. Still, how she called my name. As if—

He leads me back to the living room. The baby's playing on the floor. Drooling.

He pays no attention to the baby. He sits on the sofa. Looks up. "You all right?"

As if she was sorry.

"Major?"

"What?"

"Go ahead and sit down."

I take an overstuffed chair and put the plate on the armrest.

"She's had a series of affairs. Nothing very serious. Even during Paulie. But he didn't mind. He loved his science. She loved her revolution. She'd see one man for awhile. Then another. It was safe with Paulie. But he wasn't enough. Not exciting for her, I guess."

The beer bottle has no label. Illegal. Looking for a little excitement. Nothing serious.

"Sorry. Did you need a glass?"

"No." A foamy cold gulp. Bitter aftertaste. The beer nearly comes up again. I put the bottle on the table. Take a very small bite of sandwich. Amazed that the chicken's so good.

"The way Pearcy was killed worries me. Not for me. Not particularly for Tennyson, but for you, Major. There's something personal about what this murderer is doing." His gaze wanders to my left. "Jenny! Call Dudley!"

Something heavy bumps the back of my chair. Head, large as a bowling ball, in my crotch. I push it quickly away. Dull-witted, friendly amber eyes. Mottled pelt. Pink washcloth of a tongue.

"Don't let him get in your lap. He still thinks he's a puppy. If he bothers you, just slap him."

Paw the size of a salad plate on my knee.

Vanderslice says, "Down. Get down."

The dog lowers the paw. Looks at Vanderslice.

"Down."

Chastened, the dog pads over to the baby.

"So what do you think?"

Don't know what to think. Spying on me. But then she called my name.

"I know Earth's trying to get at you, but why? And they're going about it in such an indirect way. It's almost as though there's some private bad blood between you and this murderer."

Dudley lies down by the toddler. Yawns. Yellow scimitar teeth. But dull eyes. Soft eyes. Not as dangerous, not as shrewd, as the leopards.

"When I asked for an HF team, I wondered who they'd send. It's no secret that Earth has had it in for her colonies for a long time. Earth isn't liked here very much, Major."

The dog holds the baby down with a powerful paw. Control. That's what Tal wants. That's what she's after. She came to the house to control me. But then—how her face changed. It changed. Maybe she was angry this morning because I controlled her. Maybe that's all.

"But when they sent you, I was incredulous. I had possibly the best psychic alive, the most famous investigator and one of the three constructs in existence. They rounded up the best team they could find. Now they're trying to destroy you. Why would they do that?"

Sweater neck caught in the dog's teeth, the baby is dragged, giggling, across the carpet. Vanderslice sniffs the air. "Jen! Poo's got doodles!"

A muted reply.

"Jen! Please!"

Vanderslice's wife bursts into the room. Hands on hips. Exasperated. "I'm working." Syllables clipped. Sharp. Not singsong Tennyson. The precise, no-nonsense cadence of Earth.

"Oh, please. Come on. I've got company."

She studies me. Bonbon eyes. Fleshy, expressive lips. Wry smirk. Not at all how I imagined Vanderslice's wife.

"Honey? This is Major Holloway."

She walks across the carpet. Shoves a hand in my face. I take it automatically. She's not smiling. "Heard a lot about you."

"Jenny? I told him about the revolution and everything."

"Jesus, John."

"No. It's okay. He's okay."

Doesn't trust me. She drops my hand. Picks up the baby. Tosses a "Nice meeting you" over her back. Her body sways as she walks. Good ass. Straight spine. Haughty. Can understand why he loves her. An M-9 walk. Reminds me of—

"So. When this is all over, what are you going to do?" he asks. "You surely won't be going back to Earth."

Haven't thought about it. Time runs in days. The next. And the next. Eighteen months of short futures.

"I have a job for you here."

But he forgets. Colonial Security is after us. There is no next week. No tomorrow. Just hours.

"Come on. I want to show you something."

I follow him back into the kitchen. Vanderslice touches a wall. It slides open. We walk out onto the patio together. And my heart stops. His backyard is full of stars.

The meadow is a vast dark sea. Far away the twinkling, jeweled shore of Hebron. At my feet lights shine in the sweet-smelling lawn.

Like a trip I took once. That's right. My mother's sister's funeral. The wide sweep of the Russian steppes, white around me. Like the black around me now. The pregnant, humid smell of snow. How I wished the cabin behind me out of existence, until I was a warm pulsing dot in the void.

Dizzy, I turn. Beside me the black silhouette of Vanderslice. He drops to the ground. For a heartbeat I think he's been shot. But then he swings his arms, his legs. And laughs. When he stands, he's glowing. A black snow-angel his shadow.

He strokes light down my sleeve. My hand. I lift phosphorescent fingers.

"We used to do this when I was a kid."

If I had grown up here, I'd be so different. Quiet clear stars above, moist stars below.

Pale ghost of Vanderslice floats the lawn. Black footprints in its wake. I follow. We sit on humpbacked boulders, islands in a night-reflected sea.

"I don't know what Earth is after," he says.

"Battle and Popek. What were they working on?"

The dog trots through the golden square of the kitchen doorway. In the yard, in the stars, it tumbles and rolls.

"Viable pairs."

A phantom dog lopes over. Nuzzles at Vanderslice's feet. He reaches down a radiant hand to stroke it.

"And Golden Thompson?" I ask.

"The construction of space."

Where sky meets earth, the lights of Hebron wink. "I don't understand."

"About viable pairs? Or why that would be important to the bombings?"

"Both."

Such peace here. Nothing deadly moving in the dark. How can he think about murder?

"See, particles have opposites. They're created out of nothingness that way. It's always going on, you know, viable pairs materializing in and out of existence like popcorn or something. Then some particles get enough energy to stick around. But when they do, they're always linked.''

The phosphorescence of the yard. Thick and teeming as the subatomic world.

"If one ceases to exist, the other does, too.''

A knot in my throat. "What?''

"Born together. Die together. If one particle is swallowed by a black hole, for example, the other is destroyed. See? It all goes back to the nature of particles. Aharanov—he was an Earther—thought that particles behave haphazardly because no two systems have identical futures. I don't know how else to explain it, but time is a macrocosmic thing. It doesn't exist on the subatomic level. So. That's the premise we've been working with for three centuries. Battle appears to have expanded beyond Aharanov.''

The dog leaps up, dashes aross the lawn. This time it comes to me, a glowing moon in its mouth.

"He wants to play fetch.''

I grab the moon. Foam ball. Very chewed. Slightly damp. I toss it.

"Battle figured that viable pairs emerge from a place where there is no time. So far, so good. But when the pairs burst into existence, that link to timelessness is never broken. Those particles are always joined, even though there may be a universe between them. They're joined at the hip by a timelessness he called null-space.''

I must not have played the game right. The dog trots around the edge of a boulder. Black swallows him. "Is he right?''

"I'm not sure. He and Popek were working on their

proofs to null-space, but they were paranoid about theft. When I got into their DEEPs, their programs self-destructed.''

Something materializes on the rock. A pillar of moonlight. The dog. ''What if you could travel through null-space?''

''Oh, in theory you could, of course. It's all on the subatomic level, Major.''

''Battle and Popek's peer reviewer was Golden Thompson. A cosmologist. Think about that. If you could step into a space that was timeless, you could walk from one planet to another instantly. Couldn't you? And if Battle and Popek discovered another way to travel, that would be something for Earth to kill them for. Wouldn't it?''

He's silent.

''Pearcy said he had gone to Earth. That he entered it through the Tennyson subway tunnels. And he had an HF patch to prove it. That's why he was killed. I assumed he just found the operations room HF was using. But maybe he was smarter than I thought. Maybe he walked into the control room of a null-space door. Tell me. How did you miss the man from Colonial Security? You have a record of everyone's arrival.''

A blurred motion. Vanderslice nodding.

''And where's he staying? You must have all the hotels and rental houses covered. You know every softgun in your inventory. He has a softgun made to his specs. Vanderslice? Where did those explosives come from?''

The wind's cold. I hunch in my jacket.

''Bastards,'' Vanderslice whispers, and he sounds so odd. Sounds so heartbroken.

Why? There's a deep, quiet ecstasy. A poignant sense of loss. Doesn't he feel it? There on the horizon lights twinkle. So dark. So silent. Should be afraid. I'm not.

A sharp ache as love cuts through me, chest to back. No mother this time to call me in from the snow. Black from horizon to horizon, and stars shine in the fields. I don't want to go home again. I can't leave this place, this planet.

"Those bastards," he says. And I'm surprised to hear he's near tears. "God, Major. You must be right. Two hundred people dead. Paulie dead. Golden Thompson. Battle. Popek. All to hide the fact that Earth's been spying on her colonies."

34

By the time I return to the house, it's late. No one but Beagle up. Vanderslice has sent the subway blueprints to his net, and Beagle studies them, half-listening to my story about viable pairs.

His softgun is beside his keyboard. "You'll stay watch?"

"Yeah, yeah." He doesn't look up from the screen.

"You sure everything's locked up tight?"

"It's all right, Dyle. Go to sleep. If anyone comes I'll hear him."

I want to check windows, but I get my own softgun and go to my room. I take a shower, climb under the covers. Through the blue glimmer of the window, across a dark expanse of lawn, the yellow glow from the neighboring house. Vanderslice's men watching.

Can't sleep for thinking. Affairs, but how she pulled the towel around herself afterwards. No Tennysonian ever had her like I did. Heard it from the whores after Lila. And not just whore talk, not like the cheap whore talk in the alleys.

Do you always do that? one asked me.

I didn't understand.

Make love like that? Do you always?

But I thought that was the way it was done.

She laughed. Laughed. Thought she was laughing at me. But then, *Christ . . . what's your name again?*

Dyle.

Christ, Dyle. You don't fuck. You fucking worship.

Dressed and out of her apartment before I understood. Told me I was good. And I wasn't even trying. Didn't matter. Never went back. Never had the same whore twice. But always that pleased surprise.

I don't care how many men Tal's had. I never cared about the men before me that Lila knew. I'm good. I'm better. Cold to me this morning, but later how she called my name. Like a cat at the bars.

Make her beg. Make her come to me this time. Stupid. No time for games. Not after eighteen months.

I'll go to her. Want to hold her so bad. Not just the sex, but the warmth. Doesn't she feel that? We'll talk. So much I don't know.

The creak of the door startles me. Footsteps on carpet. The door rumbles as it closes.

Tal. Thinks I'm asleep. Let her wake me up. Want to see how she—

Something heavy sits on the bed. Heavier than Tal. Beagle? No. He'd say something.

Colonial Security. The man with Reece's face. Destroyed Beagle in the living room with . . . with what?

My softgun. Left it in the bathroom. Reece. Sitting on the end of my bed with a knife. Waiting for me to wake up.

I could shout. Hear me through the windows. Vander-slice's men running across the dark. In time? Would they come in time?

Tal. Got to Tal already. I sit up fast. Fists ready.

Balding head. Silver beard. Maroon pajamas. It's Szabo.

"Were you asleep?"

Catch my breath.

"I didn't wake you, did I?"

"No. I was—No."

"Hey, Dyle? I'm sorry about everything that's happened."

His back is bowed. Skin is pale. Even his eyes seem faded. What is he talking about?

"I just wanted you to know that."

"All right."

"HF asked me to watch you. You know, report back and everything. They told me you had a bad annual psych test." He shrugs. "And you seemed . . . well, you seemed . . ."

"I know."

"But, strange, isn't it? How nothing makes sense? I don't know, Dyle. Does life make any sense to you?"

Asking me? He should ask Beagle. He should ask Tal.

"I miss him."

Don't want to hear. I stare over his shoulder to that safe spot, there, on the wall.

"Eighteen months ago I would have been able to pick up on what was happening. I would have been able to see. Beagle told me what HF did. And I let them do that to me. Stood there and let them do that. Isn't that weird?

They chose me because I was the weak link.''

"Um.''

"I played right into their hands. I left Milos. Just when he needed me.''

"Well, you know how it is.''

"You never left your wife like that. Milos would never, ever have left me. We had history together. Isn't that strange? What I did, I mean? And I tried to get him out of the bus. I heard him screaming.''

"No way. It was quick. Probably didn't know what hit him.''

"Well, you're right of course. Maybe he didn't scream. Not really. Maybe his mind screamed and I heard it. I tried to save him. Well, too late for that, wasn't it? Too damned late. You think . . . Hey, Dyle? When he comes to me, I tell him, but . . . You think he knows I'm sorry?''

Dull blue eyes. Dim-witted and moist. Like Vander-slice's dog. They scare me. "How would I know?''

"Endwrapping comes and goes. I thought when they put me back into service that I was ready. They told me I was ready. The psychologist said everything was all right. I could handle seeing Milos again. But I don't know . . . When I saw him, it was so strange. So odd. I just couldn't.''

Wish he'd leave.

"Nothing makes sense. What they did to us. The whole damned world's upside down, isn't it? I thought—I hated you for a while. Did you know that?''

"No.''

"I can hide things well. When I want to. That's why you didn't know I was the plant. And isn't that strange of you, too? You're the investigator and all.''

"Szabo, look. Why don't you put on a trank and go to bed?''

Dull eyes. "But it's important.''

"What?''

"The dark. Milos says it's important.''

Tired of his craziness. Tired of his grief. "Yeah. I'll remember that.''

"Don't forget.''

"Why don't you go get some sleep?''

He gets up. "I'm sorry about everything.''

"No problem.''

He leaves. I climb out of bed. Put on shorts. A pair of slacks. Peek out the door. Szabo's gone. The house is silent but for keyboard sounds coming from the living room.

I turn the opposite way. Walk down the hall to Tal's. The door opens for me. I slip in, and it closes behind.

Dark in here. A shiver of fear up my chest, but not too bad. Coverlet on the bed is a plain of glimmering white. I stand and listen to her breathe.

The coverlet shifts. "Who's there?''

A strong woman, but I've frightened her. Should I have come? Maybe she said my name with pity.

"Who is it?''

"Me.''

"Oh.'' Just that. Nothing else. No offers. No apologies. Just that.

"Well . . .'' I hesitate. Wait for her to speak again. She doesn't. "Sorry I woke you.'' And I walk toward the door.

"You didn't wake me.''

I turn.

"What time is it?" she asks.

Wall's dark. Clock turned off. "I don't know."

"I think I fell asleep for a few minutes. But then I woke up. Restless night."

For eighteen months, my restless nights.

"Don't leave just yet." Not an offer. Not quite that. Should I climb into bed? Stand and talk?

"Turn on the bedside lamp," I tell her.

"Why?"

"I want to see you."

I hear the soft tick of the light switch. Wince while my eyes adjust. Not too bright. Just the one globe. And Tal against the pillows.

I go to her. Slide my hand under the warmth of the covers. And like a gift, her skin. Watching me. I lie down beside her, on top of the sheets. Tug the blanket from around her.

She tries to cover herself. Gently, so gently, I pull the blanket down.

"What are you doing?"

"I want to see you."

Naked in the glow of the lamp. Slip my hand across the flare of her ribcage. Strong bones.

"Tell me about yourself."

She's tense. "What do you want to know?"

"Everything."

She looks away. "Where do you want me to start?"

"The beginning."

"My parents were old-fashioned."

Waits for me to say something. But I'm speaking already.

"Are we going to make love, or what?"

"Just talk."

She sighs. "Okay. So in school, I was a terror. They taught us how to read, of course. But let us only read some things. No novels. No news. No science. A friend of mine, a boy, taught me how to hack."

My hand stops. That boy. Her first time? How old was she? I was thirteen.

"I started arguing with the teachers. My parents found out. But I'd already figured out what was happening. The way our world was. That others were different. They tried to teach us knitting. Do you believe it? And sewing. Didn't make any sense to me, when we could just go to the store and buy things. They wanted to keep us occupied."

The leopards. Did they resent the cage? And did they love their vet because he sometimes took them out? Maybe it wasn't the affection. Maybe it was the freedom.

Breathing harder now. Rise and fall of her chest. Pink skin, just beginning to flush. Right where my hand touches.

"Are you sure you don't want to—"

"No. Go on. Tell me."

"Okay. Let's see. I married Paulie when I was seventeen. My parents didn't know what else to do. And he was a nice man. Taught me a lot."

Column of neck. Depression below it, like a little cup.

"They shouldn't have killed him," she says, and finally, after all this time, I hear pain. "What about you?"

"Nothing about me. I'm a cop."

"What else?"

"Nothing. I'm a cop."

Her hand on the back of my neck. She pulls me to her. Lips part. The taste of her tongue. Other hand on my zipper. I take it away.

"Say it," I tell her.

She doesn't understand.

"Say it."

Ashamed. "I want you." The words are right, the tone is wrong.

"Say it." Mound of her breast. Heavier, more fleshy, than it looks. Erect nub of her nipple.

Whisper. "I want you." Her eyes. Greedy. Hand fumbles at my zipper and I let her. Then I kick my clothes away. But slow. Enter her slow. Have to teach her to hold back. To—

A sound. From outside the door. Thump of something falling. Something heavy. I raise my head.

"What's that?" she asks.

Beagle shouts, "Dyle!"

I leap away from her. My shorts. Where are my shorts?

"Dyle!" Beagle. Alarmed.

There. White wad under the bed. I pull them on. "Where's your softgun?"

"The nightstand."

"Get it. Stay here. Just stay here."

The living room is empty. All in order. Where's Beagle?

Frantic. "Dyle!"

The kitchen. Beagle kneeling on the floor beside—

Body on the tiles. Curled into a torturous comma. Fists tucked to chin. Mouth agape. Face contorted in final surprise. Feet twisted. That's what gets to me. Those naked, twisted feet.

Splash of pale on the chest of his maroon pajamas where the material fused. The softgun lies three feet away, at the door of the refrigerator. Oh, goddamn it. Beagle tried to tell me. They both did.

Bedlam of noise at the front of the house. Three men. Loud in the kitchen. Softguns in hands. They freeze when they see Szabo.

"Which one of you shot him?"

A man grabs Beagle's wrist. Pushes a tester down his palm. Another picks up the softgun and takes a reading. Their expressions relax.

A man says, "Death spasm must have been a good one for him to have flung his weapon all the way over here." He looks up. Mild face, but hard eyes. He sees my expression and looks away. "Well. I'll call the morgue."

Tal walks in, a robe around her. I stand between her and Szabo. Won't let her see. Gather my arms around her shoulder and lead her into the hall. "Go back to bed."

"What happened?"

"Nothing. Szabo killed himself. Go back to bed."

When I walk back to the kitchen, Beagle's saying, "Tell Vanderslice we want to go into the tunnels."

A man nods. "Yes, sir."

"Tell him we're going in tomorrow, with or without his help."

"I'll tell him."

The coroner comes. Beagle and I wait while they put Szabo into a bag. Until they cover those naked, twisted feet and take him away.

No. Nothing important at all.

35

Looks like a rat hole. ECCLESIASTES 6 beside it, painted a fiery warning red. God, I don't want to go down there.

Vanderslice rubs his hands together. "This is what it's all about, isn't it? The real spy game. Danger. Not knowing what to expect." Sounds like envy. Doesn't he realize? No one's better at the game than Colonial Security. No one.

Round ceiling, steep steps. And the dark. It's hot in the suit. Softgun holster is tight around my thigh. Sweating, but my fingers, my back, are ice. Beagle doesn't look like himself. Looks almost dangerous. Tight shiny suit and that helmet. But not dangerous enough.

A cartoon mouse hole. Down it, a magic door to Earth. Down it, Reece.

I brought the knife just in case. Not really Reece. But scares me like that. A little knife. Three inch blade. Easy to hide, so Beagle can't find it.

Instructions. Damn. Vanderslice has been giving instructions and I've missed—

"... nothing gets outside the suit once you put the vi-

sor down. Not body sounds, not heat. You can talk to
each other through the headsets. The suit has its own air
supply. The low-friction boots won't leave infrared.''

''Been shopping again at one of your anti-terrorist conventions?'' Beagle. Flexing his gloves. Smiling. How can
he?

There's a line of sweat above Vanderslice's lip. His
eyes are too quick. Laugh too sharp. ''Great places, those
conventions. Lots of toys. These are hard suits by the way,
besides being slippery. So if it gets into hand-to-hand
combat, you'll have the edge.''

Beside the wall: ECCLESIASTES 6. Above the hole:
DOWN.

''Good luck, Major.'' Hand shoved at me. Vanderslice.
I want to grab him. Pull him in with me. Show him what
fear's like.

Too late. Beagle starts toward the tunnel. My feet moving me. Taking me

DOWN

He's switched on the Glo-Lite. No time now. Behind
me, Vanderslice, his men. Faces somber. Want to grab
hold, so the dark won't suck me inside.

Ceiling. Three inches above the top of Beagle's helmet.
Stairway. Gloomy intestine of a place. Unused, musty
smell. And below . . .

Don't look. Watch Beagle. One turn. Another. Leave
the bright and enter cramped dusk. Not as bad as I
thought. Like twilight. Cold blue Glo in Beagle's hand.
Our shadows dance on the walls.

Fourth turn. Air basement-cool. Cave-clammy. So dark
ahead that dots swim in my eyes. Stop that. Watch Beagle.

Catacomb. A grave. Refuse of construction, like priests' skulls. What if there's an earthquake? We'd never get out. Trapped. Like the people in the subway.

"We're almost at the bottom." Beagle. Speaking quietly.

Picked up my fear, even though I'm a step behind. Hears my rapid breaths.

One more turn. An echoing, black expanse. Ecclesiastes 6 maintenance area. Christmas tree bank of lights. The brain of the section's superconductor. Huge room. Black corners too far away, beyond the reach of the Glo.

"Here." Beagle turns right.

I hurry. Walk at his side. Shoulder to shoulder. Twilight. Not so bad, but . . .

Too quiet. Can't hear his steps. There he is. Walking beside me.

"The entrance can't be in the superconductor areas. They're checked once a month. If we find it, it'll be in one of the passageways."

The only sound is Beagle's soft voice, the rasp of my breathing, and the faint drip-drip of water. Wide tunnel; high ceiling. Shoes so slippery that I have to step carefully: toe first, then heel. But not as bad as I thought it would be. I can do this. Just have to remember not to look ahead, that's all.

The tunnel widens, and there's a recess in the wall. A body-stowing place. Wait. Something's in there. A heap of dusty clothes. Corpse-yellow face. Gaping mouth . . .

"Far enough." Beagle stops and lifts the Glo. "You feeling okay?"

Just a tarp. That's all. "Yes."

"Because I'm going to turn off the Glo."

Didn't think my heart could beat faster. The light's gone. There's no up. No down. Where's Beagle? Where did he go?

"Put down your visor. Dyle! Listen to me! Put your visor down!"

Gasp and swallow darkness. Cramp in my chest. Heart attack. That's what. Christ. A heart attack. Die here in the—

Something clips me in the eye. A click.

Oh. There. In front of me. Orange and red pumpkin. Like Halloween, only . . . Beagle's face.

"What's the matter with you?" Beagle's voice. Close, tinny and in stereo.

I'm trembling. Whooping. Sweat rolls, but my hands are ice. Have to get. Have to get air. Reach for my throat, but . . . What is that?

"Dyle? Stop scratching at your visor." Beagle pushes my hands away. "What's going on?"

"Heart."

"It's not a goddamned heart attack. Dyle? You hear me? You're hyperventilating. Stop it."

Can't stop.

Orange face close to mine. Hand over—God. His hand over my air intake. Smothering me. It was Beagle. All the time. Beagle. Not Szabo.

"Lie down. That's right. Slow breaths," he says. "Even breaths."

It was Beagle. He killed Szabo. I fumble for my knife. Too late. And hands too cold. Can't hold on.

"Stop fighting. Christ, Dyle. Just lie still."

The pain eases.

"Good. That's it. That's right. Slow, even breaths."

Tired now. So tired. Maybe I'll just lie here. Maybe if I'm very still it'll all go away. After a few minutes he lifts his hand from my air intake.

"Jesus God, Dyle. Don't scare me like that."

His concerned face, a radiant heat about him. A ruddy halo of flame. He's not working for them. Of course not. Never was. And . . . Wait. What's that? Flicker on his forehead. On the left. A bright yellow pulse.

"You okay now?"

"Head's yellow."

"What?"

"Your left side. Yellow."

A blaze in the right cranium.

"Moved."

"Where?"

"Your right."

"You sure?"

What could that be? "Yes."

"Shit. I bet you can see me thinking. Left side's the Hoad Taylor half. Right side the mechanics. Expensive damned infrared. Listen. Don't get excited. I'm going to put my own visor down. Hold onto my arm. Just hold onto my arm, okay?"

Beagle winks out. The room whirls.

"Incredible. You can't even see our footsteps. You notice that?"

Can't scream. Not with a mouthful of dark. Then . . . that's better. See it now. One dull spark.

"I turned on the Glo. You can lift your visor."

Frantic. Grapple for the fastener. Click as the glass slides up. Twilight again, blue and eerie.

"We got the big guns, Dyle." He laughs. "Pretty Boy came through with the goodies."

He puts out his hand. I grab it, but it's too oily. My fingers slip.

"Slick suits. Infrared. The whole bag of goodies."

I get up and we're walking again. Toe, heel. Slippery shoes and if I forget, I'll fall. Beagle will leave me behind.

How far now? Beagle's moving too fast, and I wish he'd slow down. Tunnels. More tunnels. A recess with construction debris in it. That's all. Piled there like a . . .

We walk. It's hard to keep my balance. The back of my thighs burn. But not too bad, though. Twilight tunnels, all the same. Hypnotic, after a while. Toe, heel. But then a scalding pain up my calf.

"Wait!" He'll leave me.

But he turns. Thank God. He stops.

"Wait a minute, Beagle. Let me sit down a minute."

"Okay."

I sit on a lump of Permacrete. Beside me, a sack. Purple letters: GOD'S HOLY ORDNANCE, INC. What if I'm too tired to get up again?

Beagle's against the other wall, a useless alcove by him. A recess so deep, so black that not even the Glo can reach the end.

That's strange.

"Is that an alcove? Or another tunnel?"

Beagle turns. "Dyle! Put down your visor. Go ahead, damn it. I'll keep the Glo on."

I slide the glass down. There's the waning August

moon of Beagle's averted face, the ember of the Glo, and
. . . wait. There's a neat red road, too. It leads into the
alcove and stops dead.

"Creep paint," he says. "So old I nearly missed it.
Must only be a few fractions of a degree above the tem-
perature of the tunnel. When it gets old like that, the top
layer slows and starts to cool."

I raise my visor fast. Cold tunnel air hits my face like
frost. That blackness at the end of the alcove. Not depth.
The absence of light.

"Lower your visor."

He turns off the Glo and everything disappears. The
alcove. Beagle. Me. Darkness pounces. I slip my visor
down and I'm all right. There's that red road again.

"Game time. No lights."

Beagle's a silhouette against the red. I rise.

"Follow the creep paint. It'll lead to the stairs. That's
how the Reece look-alike gets in and out. Tell Vanderslice
to bring his troops."

The road is a dull angry crimson. Down the corridor it
fades. Fatigued, looks like, rather than distance. I want
him to go with me.

"Go on, Dyle. You have to go."

Have to. Or die. I think about that, and keep my head
down. Watch the road, the dark fissures in the paint. Here
and there fiery coals. Mesmerizing.

"Dyle!"

A shout loud in both ears. I stop. Nothing around me
but black. Red at my feet. "What?"

"Off the paint!"

"What?"

"Off the paint! Now!"

Can't leave the red. But I leave it, anyway. Walk until I bump the tunnel wall.

"You off it now? You in the shadows?"

"Yeah."

"Don't move. Someone just came out the door and he's headed your way. Dyle?"

I hear the anxiety, like a constriction in his throat. "What?"

"It's a construct."

Heart slams my sternum. Again. Again. So hard I feel my chest shudder.

"Stay out of his way. I'm tracking behind. Don't go up against him. Dyle? You listening? Don't try to stop him yourself."

God. Can't see. Can't hear anything but Beagle's voice.

"Don't use your softgun!"

Black of the wall. Red road. Leads off to—

"Dyle? Listen, goddamn it! Don't use your softgun!"

There. Coming out of the gloom. Loose-hipped, world-beating walk. Golden in the dark. Oh, for the love of God. I understand what HF did to me. Why there were no DNA markers on the bomb casings. Why the holo never caught him. Earth only reconstructed the best. The most brilliant.

Beagle, two others. And Reece Wallace.

Thoughts spark the radiance of his forehead. Left hand thoughts. Human thoughts. Of course HF sent Reece to kill Lila. They knew he'd do it right. Is he happy? Remembering? My hand goes down. Down. To the softgun. Fingers grope until I touch the edge of the knife.

Walking past me. Doesn't look. Bastard. Like I'm beneath his notice. Smiling. Like I'm not dangerous enough.

Orange gleam of Reece's head and hands. Duller red where clothes soak warmth. Dark black of a duffel bag.

Three strides past I step out behind him, moving fast. Palm under his chin and I snap his head back. He drops to his knees. Flame across his forehead. Left side. Astonishment. The duffel bag falls.

Trying to get up. His eyes frantic with questions. I plunge the blade into his socket. A wrench of the knife and the eye pops out.

Can't hear him. Feel him grunt. Does it hurt? Can anything hurt? Hands fumble on my arms. Slide off.

So damned strong. He twists. I hit the side of the tunnel. Scrabble up quick before he sees.

He whirls. Hand clamped to empty socket. Forehead ablaze. Single eye straining.

I circle. Lunge. Arm around his throat. Plunge the knife into the other socket. Blade snaps and can't hold on. It skitters across the corridor. The eye drops to his cheek. Hangs by a wire.

Flings me off hard. The wall knocks the breath from my lungs. Hears me that time. Heard me fall. He leaps. We tumble into a pile of rock.

Beagle heard me, too. That explosion of air. "What the fuck are you doing?"

Can't answer. Arms around my knees. Strong arms. Metal underneath. The suit starts to give. Going to break my legs. And what then? I claw at the rocks. Try to pull myself free. No use. Stronger than I am. Always was.

"Dyle! Goddamn it!"

He's coming. I know it. But he won't get here in time.

There. Touched something. Something big. Chunk of Permacrete. Turn and slam it into the side of Reece's head. The blow drives him backward. Arms fall away.

Ragged triangular patch of scalp hanging. Bright hot metal of the skull beneath. He reaches for me. Misses.

I lift the rock. Bring it down. Metal bends. Hit him again. Feel the jolt up my shoulder.

Damn. He's trying to get away. Tremor through his fingers. Shudder up his back. It feels so good. I sit back and watch him crawl.

He hits the wall and stops. Gropes. Drags himself, blind, down the corridor. One arm useless. Sparks like fireworks in the open brain. Too easy, damn it. He is dying too easy.

Rises to one knee. Sways. Right arm limp. Left brain dark ruby. All the Reece gone. What's left of him struggles down the creep paint. Crimson friction behind him, like blood.

I get up. Follow. Lift the rock. Bring it down. Despite the metal, a fragile skull. Under my hands he squirms. Blind, deaf, he tries to escape, and ends up at the wall.

I bring the rock down. Knock him off balance. Wires spill, and pieces of plastic. Orange streamers and red confetti. His nails rake the ground.

Hit him. Hit him. Christ. For Lila. For everything. I hit him until I can't lift the rock anymore.

Head below me dull orange. Flattened oval. When did he stop moving? How long has it been?

"Dyle."

Beagle. On the ruby creep paint. On the bright orange

of Reece's struggle. A dark Archangel with a red coal in
its hand.

"Jesus God, Dyle." A whisper loud as judgment.

I raise my visor and the world hits me full in the face.
By my side, an outrage. Looks like a man. Even looks
vulnerable. Those arms twisted under him. The sprawled
legs. I search for the blood on me. Should have blood,
with his head smashed like that.

"It's not my fault," I tell Beagle. Metal and silicon and
wires. Not really a death. And it didn't feel good enough
to be murder. I wanted blood on my hands. Wanted to
hear him scream.

"He killed Lila."

Beagle says, "I know."

"Don't look at me like that, damn it! It's just a fucking
machine." Beagle looks hurt. But nothing can hurt him.
Just silicon. Just wires. "Besides, he attacked me first."
And the lie is out before I can stop it.

"You okay?"

"I'm fine. I'm just fine."

Not really. I get up. Body at my feet. His face. God.
His face. Sharp shiny metal underneath. All that effort,
and no pain.

A hand touches my shoulder. Just once, and very
briefly. I turn, but no one's there. Not now. Not ever
again.

36

Vanderslice, legs crossed, sits in a floral overstuffed chair. On the desk lies Reece's severed head. No one looks at it. I do. I force myself to look.

Artificial bogeyman, memories buried in metal, under synthetic flesh. Red bundles of fiber optics. Yellowish mock fat. The mouth is torn. Teeth missing. No blood, damn it. No blood. But still, the lips are open in surprise.

I stare until my eyes burn. Until my stomach does a slow, queasy roll. My hands are clenched so hard that they cramp. So hard that fingernails dig into flesh. I understand now how far HF was willing to go. The planning it took. We'll never make it out alive. Colonial Security will find us eventually. Hunt us, one by one. They have all the time in the world.

I let my eyes drift to the chair behind, to the slumped figure of Marvin. A minister clears his throat. Marvin doesn't look up.

"Excellency?" Vanderslice asks.

Marvin lifts his head. His face is marshmallowy from insomnia. But his eyes are sharp. "Gentlemen. The end time is nigh."

A clink as a minister fumbles his coffee cup, but Beagle's quiet. He's looking at Reece's crushed skull.

Beagle's expression is thoughtful, as if he's contemplating his own mortality, that metal under the skin. Just a machine, I told him. Not really murder. And he cut the head off, not me.

Marvin says, "Harold the first Chosen commanded us: if thy brother sin, smite him. It is written that at the end time the good brother will lift hand against his evil twin."

Beagle cut off his head.

"The righteous blow will smite the demon into the dust." Marvin's tiny eyes. Agate eyes. They meet mine and I feel his strange intensity. "God has laid his hands on us to fulfill the prophecy, gentlemen. We must rise up and smite Earth."

No. Insanity.

"Uh . . ." from a chair near the fireplace. A short man with a frog-like face has raised a hand.

"Yes, Kreger?"

Kreger licks his lips. "Begging your pardon, Your Excellency, but we only have two armed ships, and those are designed to be defensive."

"A paltry army," Marvin says. "That was what Harold the First told us of the end time. A paltry army, a glorious victory. With God at your side, there's no need for fear. Go to your Transportation Ministry and pick out your followers."

Christ. What's Marvin doing? He'll give Colonial Security an excuse to invade. Can't he see we have to buy time? He's crazy. Like Szabo with the softgun. Crazy like that.

Kreger says, "It pains me, Your Excellency, but the defensive ships aren't designed for the event horizon. They're a border patrol."

"Perhaps we can arm some transports," Marvin says.

Stupid. Lives in a dream world. Vanderslice was right. How did I think Tennyson could survive? This whole damned planet, a dream world.

Kreger slouches, makes himself a smaller target. "Even if we managed to get armed transports through the event horizon, Your Excellency, it would take my men a couple of hours to get reoriented after jump sleep. By the time we woke up, Earth would have surrounded us. They'd be waiting and they'd . . ."

Stars in their night fields. Houses and green lawns. That's how these people grew up. Not shoulder to shoulder. Not fighting for room, never listening for footsteps. Grew up trusting the dark.

"Maybe we could send a strongly-worded communiqué instead."

Quickly, everyone looks toward Marvin.

He links his hands on the desk. "If we cannot go to Earth, we will bring Earth to us. Kreger. Get what ships you have readied and set them outside our end of the singularity. Sanderson, have your Communications Ministry send a declaration of war. As the Earth ships fly through, we will smash them."

Which one is Sanderson? The man with the weak blue eyes? He could be pushed. The dark-headed one? He looks cocky enough.

"A declaration of war?" Tall, thin man. Long legs, like a spider. "To Earth, Your Excellency?"

A crack. Marvin slaps his hand on the desk and stands. His face is incipient-embolism red. "Of course, Earth! Gentlemen, please. We must strike now, lest God consider us weak-willed!"

Sanderson regards the head of Reece Wallace. That's right. Look at it good. Think what memories that brain case contained. Think about that.

"Go. Send our demand for unconditional surrender to Earth."

A skittish laugh escapes. Then Sanderson clamps his fingers over his mouth. "You're joking, right, Your Excellency? I mean, don't you see that we'd never have a chance?"

"If you haven't the stomach for it, just say so."

Sanderson untangles his legs. Getting up. If he leaves the room—if he obeys that order—

"Respectfully, sir. I can't," he says. The other ministers watch him leave.

"Kreger?"

At the brink now. At the edge. Only takes one of them to say yes.

But Kreger gets to his feet as well. "You're forcing me to choose between the safety of the people I represent and the religion I've dedicated my life to."

"What we are faced with is the choice between flesh and spirit, Kreger. I don't ask you to choose. God does."

Kreger's eyes search the room, and meet mine. Does he see me sweating? Does he understand what that means? Nervous, he looks away. "Your Excellency? If we war against Earth, Earth will win. I just can't do this."

Kreger walks away fast and Marvin lifts his head to the

ceiling. Toward mute Heaven. "Which of you has faith? Carney?"

Older man with white hair. He pulls himself wearily to his feet. "Thank you, sir. I'll hand in my resignation in the morning."

Carney, a strange attractor, pulls the rest of the crowd after him.

"John!"

At Marvin's anguished shout, Vanderslice stops, his hand on the door, me at his side.

"Peter might have denied Christ, but John was faithful. I've always thought of you as my own beloved John. Did you know that?"

Vanderslice doesn't turn. His face is bloodless. And I'm glad when he walks out the door. There's too much destruction in that room. Marvin. Reece. Everything a ruin.

37

Toe, heel. Dark figures ahead on the crimson, like cooler spots in lava. Beagle beside me. No sound but the whispers of breathing.

Dull red road and darkness. And then—What's that? Hot orange streaks in the red. Yellow scuff marks where something was dragged. One clear handprint. Reece's. As he tried to crawl away.

"You all right?"

Beagle's voice. A giant black silhouette against the road.

Ahead, someone stops and turns. Slender body. Duffel bag. Not Reece. Vanderslice.

"I'm fine."

That handprint. Just a machine. The way he trembled. Like Tal trembled under me. Didn't die easy this time. Toyed with him. Until his face changed. But it wasn't good enough.

"Dyle?" Beagle.

"Yeah, yeah. I'm okay."

Toe, heel. Toe, heel.

"Sir?"

Vanderslice's "Yes?"

"We've arrived at the door. Taking up positions along the alcove. No activity as yet."

Ahead, a black knot of men, flaws in ruby. Not as far as I remembered it, then.

A guard's voice. "All clear."

Sparks in the gloom now. The Glos.

I take off my helmet to twilight. Slender man in a dark suit. Curly hair. Vanderslice. I crouch next to him as he sets up equipment. Beagle slumps against the opposite wall.

"Do or die time, Major." Vanderslice unrolls the flex monitor, props it atop the transmitter.

Do and die.

Beagle fondles the bomb. His eyes have lost their focus. I know what he's doing. Counting down to zero. I've done it before. Repeating last minute instructions, a liturgy, a Hail Mary. Get in. Set the bomb. Get out.

Vanderslice fits a lead into the monitor. "Gene?"

A blond guard looks around. "Sir?"

"Everything set at my house?"

"Yes, sir."

"You'll get word to them if something goes wrong? They'll take the EPAT out? Get her and the baby away?"

"Yes, sir. Don't worry about that, sir."

Vanderslice's eyes on me. I've finally seen him scared. And I don't like it. Then he snaps in the last lead. "Ready."

Beagle puts on his helmet and starts to the door. I leap to my feet. "Hoad!" I call him by name. By his name. And in my voice—

He turns. Want to see his eyes again. But can't, not through the helmet.

"Let me go with you."

"You'd mess up my timing."

Just for once, I need to see them beaten. "I want—"

"Goddamn it, Dyle. Don't play your power games with me. I said I can handle it. And we aren't sure the door isn't booby-trapped now."

Hurt him. Pricked his vanity.

He waits. But what do I want to say? If I can't go, do it for me. Do it right. "Get back here quick. Four minutes. Remember."

"Three minutes fifty nine seconds." He walks around the edge of the alcove, trailing the camera wire.

Vanderslice kneels by the monitor. I crouch beside him. The guards shuffle backward, set up a new defensive perimeter.

Beagle's inside. On the screen is a bright room. White room. Full of Colonial Security. They're frozen in the first stage of surprise.

Camera lowers. Beagle's huge form steps into view. "Please stay where you are. The bomb has a limited range."

Anxiety sweeps the crowd like gossip. A tech drops a Sheet. White-haired man steps forward. Stops short when Beagle raises the softgun.

"You can't set off a bomb in here," the man says, and he sounds so panic-stricken that I start to smile.

Beagle edges toward the camera. His hand drops out of view. An empty click. Then another. A breathy, "Shit."

Across the bottom of the monitor time unravels in blue.

Two minutes, fifty-nine seconds.

"Vanderslice?" Beagle's voice. Like a newscaster reporting on a remote disaster. "The floor's too slick. The suction cups won't grab."

"Try it again, Dr. Taylor."

Beagle kneels. Click.

Two minutes, twenty-one seconds.

The white-haired man whirls to a female technician. "Shut down the null-door!"

She lunges toward the controls. We lose the feed. Image dances, flips crazily. Then . . . tech on the ground. Fists to chest. Face surprised. He killed her. Beagle killed her. Thank God. Was afraid he wouldn't have it in him. Didn't think—

One minute, forty-eight seconds.

"Listen!" The white-haired man. Face red with anger. "This is a no-weapons room, you understand? No explosives. No softguns."

Colonial Security men huddle in a corner. Helpless. Impotent. The bastards. Of course. I understand. No softguns. Beagle tears the helmet off. His jowls droop over the tight collar of his suit.

"The door exists in null-space," the man says. "If you add energy to one side, you open a temporary pathway. Vacuums are inherently unstable . . ."

Vanderslice half-rises. Screams, "Shut off the bomb!"

The shout must have been deafening. A flinch. The softgun lowers. A flicker of movement to Beagle's left and the screen dissolves.

I grab for Vanderslice, for the mike. He pulls away in surprise. "Let Beagle do it!" I shout.

Kill them all. That's what I want. They're so afraid. Must set up a backblast, that's why. Can't let Vanderslice stop him now. Feels too good. I fumble for the mike, to tell him—

Then a guard wrestles me away.

On the screen. Picture flips. Clears. Two Colonial Security men down. Trash can rolling away from the corpses.

I struggle, reach out. Want to tell Beagle—"Let him do it!"

Fifty-six seconds.

Vanderslice says, "Dr. Taylor! Disarm that bomb!"

Beagle looks into the camera, his face so close that I can see the broken capillaries in his cheeks. Seventeen seconds.

"Dyle? I—" A whisper so quiet he might have been speaking to himself.

Do it. Goddamn. Do it. For Lila. For me.

Four seconds. Waiting until the last instant. Has to. Or they'll push the bomb through to our side.

"The red lead!" Vanderslice. Terrified and frustrated. His fists pummel his thighs. "The red lead!"

Two seconds.

Thank God. Beagle will.

One.

It happens suddenly. And all in silence. Quiet as the palace coup. Bloodless as that. The monitor is black.

I'm laughing. The guard lets me go. I jump up. Run to the alcove. Want to tell him how good it felt.

A body. There, in the shadows. He's fallen. Beagle's hurt. No. Just a tarp. A pile of rubble. A severed strand of wire. And three blank Permacrete walls.

"Major?" Vanderslice behind me.

The door's gone. But where's Beagle? Oh, that's what he's doing. He's hiding. That's all. Playing a game. Wants to scare me. But nothing can scare me anymore.

"Beagle?" My voice quakes with laughter. "Hey, Beagle!"

Blank gray wall. Severed wire. And no one answers.

"God." Vanderslice's whisper, like a knife.

I turn. There are tears in his eyes.

38

Clear night. Steady wind. If I close my eyes I imagine I smell the sea. But over the tips of my boots, the glittering necklace of Hebron and a carpet of stars.

A four-legged glowing shape emerges from the star field. When the dog reaches me, he plants his paws on the chaise lounge and shoves his nose into my crotch. I laugh and push him away.

The dog's warm. And insistent. A scrabble of his back legs. He lies down, side to my warm side. Head crooked in my arm.

I scratch under his chin. He pushes against my hand. Greedy. "Damned pain in the ass," I murmur. "Dudley? Hear me? You're a goddamned pain in the ass."

I raise my eyes and follow the glowing trail of a transport, a slow shooting star. Track it until it's blotted out by a dark shape between me and the sky.

"Hi." The only phosphorescence on the shadow is what splattered on his legs during the walk from his house. Since Vanderslice lost his innocence, he doesn't play his childhood game anymore..

He sits on a chair next to me, in the rectangle of light

from the kitchen. "Hey. Bodyguard. Enjoying your vacation?"

I stretch.

"I'll keep you busy when you come back. Full itinerary." He pauses. "You know, I want to promote you some day. Maybe as Minister of Internal Safety. But I want you to learn to relax a little . . ."

"I understand."

"Dyle? I can't have Tennyson become like—"

"I understand." Still afraid of me. And maybe he should be. I grew up wrong. "I'm happy with what I'm doing." Stars in my own fields. Nothing, not even memories, moving in the dark.

He clears his throat. "Where's Tal?"

"Left about an hour ago." Still sore from her. A good sort of pain. "She never stays long."

"Well, she's dedicated to her causes." He pities me. But he shouldn't. No one else loves her like I do. When I let her out of the cage, she gives me the best part. I take her inhibitions. I change her face.

He says, "The third probe came back today."

Above us, emptiness. On the horizon, Hebron. More beautiful, and easier to love, from a distance. Everything is.

"The scientists are divided. Some think the moon will leave the solar system. Some think it will eventually become a satellite of Jupiter."

I press my cheek against the top of Dudley's head. The moon off on a search for its missing mate. No, it won't stop for Jupiter.

"We resettled the people from Moon Base on Turner's

World. They wouldn't have wanted to come here, I guess.''

For a transcendent moment, we were magicians. Now you see that blue ball in the sky. Now you don't. Nothing but desperation up our sleeves.

A chuckle. ''I retrieved some HF files from the moon and found a story you'll like.''

I turn on my side, toward Vanderslice. Dudley resettles himself with a grunt, lifts a proprietorial leg over my chest. I let it stay.

''Before he was reconstructed, Hoad Taylor worked on a case where a man was strangling young boys. Maybe you remember. After killing them, he . . . uh, voided his bowels over the dead bodies.''

''He shit on their faces. Ivan Carr. I remember reading about that.''

Vanderslice pries at a bottle. The distinctive smell of Tennysonian beer drifts on the breeze.

''So when they arrested him, Taylor comes bursting into the interrogation room. Carr was cuffed with his hands behind him. So Taylor asks the guy's name. The suspect gets to the 'I' in Ivan, and Taylor slams this . . . uh, piece of excrement, into Carr's mouth. Everybody's shouting, and the suspect is trying to get away. But Taylor makes him swallow it. Some of the witnessing officers swore it was Taylor's own, well, turd I suppose is the appropriate word here.''

I listen to Vanderslice's lonely laughter. When it's over, I say, ''Dog crap.''

''Oh. He tell you the story?''

"Beagle would have thought his shit was too good for Carr."

He seems hurt that I don't find his story funny. The wind dies. The malt smell of beer lies heavy on the air. One step backward. That's all it would have taken, and he had everything timed. One step, but he couldn't. Easier to die than face aftermaths.

"John. Don't you understand? Everything Beagle did was premeditated. He waited. And then made Earth swallow his shit."

Vanderslice shakes his head. "He didn't know what he was doing."

"He knew." I lift my mug from the table. Take a sip. The coffee's cold. "You find out how he died?"

"Early onset Alzheimer's."

The answer's so fitting, so sad, that it makes me shiver.

"Dr. Taylor knew what he would die of from childhood. It was there in his DNA scan. Before the symptoms started, HF downloaded him. A few years later he started forgetting the access code to his apartment. The logon to his net. Then his criminology patterns started showing up with holes in them, stupid mistakes he should have caught. Irascibility is one of the symptoms. HF tried to get him to retire, but he refused to acknowledge what was happening. He stayed on, trying to work."

"Did he opt for Release?"

"Release forms require that you be sound of mind, remember? They eventually euthanized him."

For five months I've thought he destroyed Earth for us. For Tennyson. Or even for what was right. But maybe Beagle had reasons of his own.

Dyle. I—

I'm sorry.

Vanderslice gets up. "Well. Better be going. Got a speech to prepare and ad spot to record." Dudley jumps from the chair, nearly dumping me over.

I steady myself. "How's the election coming?"

"God. Tal doesn't understand that change takes time. She actually threatened me. Can you believe that? Said that if I didn't get her demands passed this first term, she'd withdraw her support next election and run herself." He laughs, and I don't like the sound of it. "Well, we're not ready for that sort of thing here, are we? Besides, she has all those political liabilities."

Me. A political liability. Can't bring herself to marry. Doesn't want that cage, no matter how large and how comfortable I could make it. But she can't stop seeing me, either.

He sighs, runs a hand through his curly hair. "Everybody at each other's throats. Bickering. Outright fights. Democracy's a pain in the butt. I should keep this planet a dictatorship."

He knows I wouldn't let him. That's the very reason he hired me. "You're kidding."

A nervous pause. His eyes shift. "Only a little."

He scratches Dudley on the head. He won't fire me now. Scared of what I'd do. And still wise enough to be scared of how power might change him. "Think you'll win?" I ask.

"I'm ahead in the polls. And I've got a lot of important people helping my campaign." The glow from the kitchen illuminates that disarming, photogenic smile. "You see, I know where all the spitballs are buried.''

He walks away. A few yards into the stars, he pauses. "It wasn't your fault. You didn't make him do it. He didn't understand what would happen. It's easier to believe that.''

He knew. That's why he didn't want me with him. I was afraid he wouldn't have the heart to kill, yet he murdered them. Every single one.

"Dyle? It's easier.''

An indecisive moment. Then Vanderslice turns and ambles off.

Doesn't he realize? Beagle was the smartest of us all. The loss of his brilliance haunted him. HF hurt him. Omniscience must have made him feel safe. *Dyle? I—*

And when it came to winning, nothing stood in his way.

I remember how time ran out, and shut my eyes hard against the last sight of that face.

Dyle? I have to.

Those sad gray eyes. Those cheeks like fallen angels.